All her life she'd been cautious and inhibited, and after her brief, disastrous relationship with Neil she'd felt frozen through and through, certain she'd never feel the warmth of true love, the pleasure of being held in caring arms.

Now, however, her inhibitions gone—driven away by the unaccustomed whisky, perhaps—she longed to reach out and take the happiness that Ross seemed to be offering.

But suppose she was frigid, as Neil had charged?

Ross had been watching her face, the changing expressions, and now, with a slight sigh, he released her arms and stepped back.

His voice level, he told her, "Don't worry. I'll take the couch...."

He was turning to walk away when she whispered, "Don't go. Please don't go."

Dear Reader,

Harlequin Presents® is all about passion, power and seduction, oodles of wealth and abundant glamour. This is the series of the rich and the superrich. Private jets, luxury cars and international settings that range from the wildly exotic to the bright lights of the big city! We want to whisk you away to the far corners of the globe and allow you to escape and indulge in a unique world of unforgettable men and passionate romances. There is only one Harlequin Presents®, available all month long. And we promise you the world….

As if this weren't enough, there's more! More of what you love…. Two weeks after the Presents® titles hit the shelves, four Presents® EXTRA titles join them! Presents® EXTRA is selected especially for you—your favorite authors and much-loved themes have been handpicked to create exclusive collections for your reading pleasure. There's anther excuse to indulge! Midmonth, there's always a new collection to treasure—you won't want to miss out.

Harlequin Presents®—still the original and the best!

Best wishes,

The Editors

Lee Wilkinson

THE BOSS'S FORBIDDEN SECRETARY

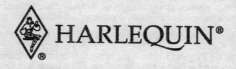

HARLEQUIN®

TORONTO • NEW YORK • LONDON
AMSTERDAM • PARIS • SYDNEY • HAMBURG
STOCKHOLM • ATHENS • TOKYO • MILAN • MADRID
PRAGUE • WARSAW • BUDAPEST • AUCKLAND

PLEASE RECYCLE
THIS PRODUCT IS RECYCLABLE

Recycling programs
for this product may
not exist in your area.

ISBN-13: 978-0-373-12815-0
ISBN-10:   0-373-12815-0

THE BOSS'S FORBIDDEN SECRETARY

First North American Publication 2009.

Copyright © 2009 by Lee Wilkinson.

www.eHarlequin.com

Printed in U.S.A.

All about the author...
Lee Wilkinson

LEE WILKINSON attended an all girls school, where her teachers, often finding her daydreaming, declared that she "lived inside her own head," and that is still largely true today. Until her marriage she had a variety of jobs, ranging from PA to departmental manager to modeling swimsuits and underwear.

An only child and an avid reader from an early age, Lee began writing when she, her husband and their two children moved to Derbyshire, U.K. She started with short stories and magazine serials before going on to write romances for Harlequin®.

A lover of animals, Lee adopted a rescue dog named Thorn after losing Kelly, her adored German shepherd. Thorn looks like a pit bull and acts like a big softy, apart from when the postman calls. Then he has to be restrained, otherwise he goes berserk and shreds the mail.

Traveling has always been one of Lee's main pleasures, and after crossing Australia and America in a motor home and traveling round the world on two separate occasions, she still, periodically, suffers from itchy feet.

She enjoys walking and cooking, log fires and red wine, music and the theater, and still much prefers books to television—both reading and writing them.

CHAPTER ONE

CATHY had packed the car, said goodbye to her neighbours, handed in the keys of the flat and set off from London that morning.

Because it was such a long way to drive, and Carl had been anxious about her, she had agreed to break the journey with an overnight stay at Ilithgow House, a small, family-run hotel that, according to the blurb, was both comfortable and inexpensive.

Carl had warned her, 'Get as early a start as possible, Sis. It's a hell of a long way just going as far as Ilithgow, and you'll have the pre-Christmas traffic to contend with.'

But, in spite of his warning, the journey had taken far longer than she had anticipated, and it had already been dark for several hours.

She had just crossed the border from England into Scotland when it started to snow. The first big, soft flakes swirled past, caught in the golden beam of the car's headlights and plopping onto the windscreen where the busy wipers flicked them carelessly aside.

Since she had been a small child Cathy had loved snow, and she thought how pretty it looked and how lovely it would be to have a white Christmas.

Or rather how lovely it *would* have been, if she hadn't, for Carl's sake, been planning to live a lie.

Peering through the windscreen, she thought thankfully that it was just as well she was almost there. The feathery flakes had grown smaller and more compact, and the snow was now coming down in earnest.

Pre-warned that there had already been fairly heavy falls in northern Scotland and over the mountains, she had expected to run into it sooner or later. But not this far south, and she was thankful that she was using Carl's four-wheel drive.

By the time she caught sight of the lighted sign that gave the name of the hotel, a rising wind had created blizzard conditions, and she was driving through a blinding curtain of white.

Turning left between the lighted gateposts, she slowed to a crawl, cheering herself with the thought that there couldn't be more than a few hundred yards to go.

Ilithgow House, she had learnt when she booked, was less than a quarter of a mile from the main road. However, to get to it she would have to cross an old stone bridge that spanned the River Ilith.

Remembering that made her hastily bring the car to a halt. She had no idea whether the long drive was straight or winding, and in these conditions it would be only too easy to miss the bridge and drive into the river.

A few seconds' thought convinced her that her best plan would be to get out and reconnoitre.

Her hand was on the door handle when, from behind, approaching headlights lit up the falling snow. A big car—a Range Rover, she thought—drew up alongside, and a man's dark figure appeared at her window.

As she rolled down the window, he stooped and, in a pleasant, low-pitched voice, asked, 'Need any help?'

Briefly she explained her predicament.

'Luckily I know the lie of the land,' he said briskly, 'so I'll lead the way, if you'd like to follow me?'

Before she had time to thank him, he had gone back to his car.

As he drove slowly ahead she followed the red glow of his tail-lights until they had bumped their way across a narrow, humpbacked bridge.

Then, through the blizzard of white, she spotted the welcoming sight of the hotel's lighted windows.

A moment later the leading car signalled right and, pulling onto a snow-shrouded forecourt, came to a halt near a shallow flight of steps.

As Cathy drew up alongside, the man doused his headlights and, jumping out, turned up the collar of his short car coat.

Though she couldn't make out his features, in the light spilling from the long windows she could see that he was tall and broad-shouldered.

Reaching to open her car door, he queried, 'I presume you've booked at the hotel?'

'Yes.'

Noticing her medium-heeled suede court shoes, he advised, 'It's getting quite nasty underfoot. You'll need to be careful.'

'Yes,' she agreed ruefully. 'I should have worn something more sensible, but I wasn't expecting to run into snow quite this soon.'

He was bareheaded, and, realizing that snowflakes were settling fast on his fair hair, she climbed out rather too hastily and slipped.

Catching her arm, he steadied her.

She pulled a face. 'Now you can say, what did I tell you?'

He laughed. 'As if I would! Have you much luggage to take in?'

'Just an overnight bag.'

When she had retrieved it from the boot, he said, 'Let me,' and took it from her.

The bag she had packed had been a fun present from Carl, and had gold-coloured teddy bears prancing on it, but if the stranger noticed, it didn't seem to bother him.

'Thank you,' she murmured. 'But don't you have your own luggage to carry?'

'I haven't any luggage. I wasn't intending to make an overnight stop. However, a rescheduled business meeting meant a late start, and, given the weather conditions, it seems preferable to possibly ending up in a ditch.'

She could only agree as, heads bent against the driving curtain of snow, they mounted the steps.

Seeing she was having a struggle to keep her footing, he put a strong arm around her. The caring gesture brought a glow of comforting warmth, in sharp contrast to the bleakness she had lived with for a long time now.

Since her parents' untimely death she had been forced to shoulder all the responsibility, and it was lovely to feel cherished and protected, to have someone else safely in control.

She was sorry when they reached the door and he took his arm away.

He rang the bell, as a small notice requested, and, turning the knob, ushered her inside. Snowflakes whirled around them like confetti, before he closed the door again, shutting out the elements.

As they wiped their feet on the doormat, he turned down the collar of his coat and brushed melting snowflakes from his thick fair hair.

The red-carpeted foyer-cum-lounge was pleasantly cosy, with several easy chairs, a couple of small couches, an abundance of Christmas decorations and a log fire burning in the old-fashioned grate.

But all Cathy's attention was taken by the man who stood so easily at her side. It was the first time she had seen him properly, and his effect on her was immediate and powerful. With his strong, clear-cut features, his chiselled mouth and those thickly lashed, heavy-lidded eyes, he was the most attractive man she had ever seen, and she wanted to keep on looking at him.

But, she reminded herself hastily, she mustn't *allow* herself to be attracted. She must try and think herself into the role of a married woman.

A role she had only agreed to play to enable her brother to get a post as a ski instructor—an ambition he had cherished since boyhood. A role she must appear to be happy in, whereas her own short, real-life experience of being married to Neil had been anything but happy...

Becoming aware that the stranger was studying her and, judging by his expression, liking what he saw, and feeling suddenly self-conscious, she glanced hastily away.

A melted snowflake dripped off her hair and trickled down her neck, making her shiver.

'You look as if you could use this.' He fished in his pocket and handed her a folded hankie, adding, 'By the way, my name's Ross Dalgowan.'

Their eyes met briefly and hers dropped, the long, curly lashes almost brushing her cheeks. 'Mine's Cathy Richardson.'

A little shy, he thought to himself, but she had to be the most fascinating woman he'd ever set eyes on and he wanted to keep looking at her.

Despite good teeth and a flawless complexion she wasn't, strictly speaking, beautiful. Her hair was somewhere between ash-brown and blonde, her eyes were every colour but no colour, her nose was too short and her mouth was too wide. But her heart-shaped face held real character and a quiet, haunting loveliness.

As they made their way over to the reception desk she mopped at her face and hair before handing back the damp square of cambric. 'Thanks.'

'Always at your service,' he said with a white, crooked grin that made her heart lurch drunkenly, then pick up speed.

She was still trying to regain her composure when a plump, homely woman with grey hair came through a door at the rear.

Smiling at them across the polished desk, she said cheerfully, 'Good evening. I'm afraid it's a nasty night...' Then, in surprise, 'Why, it's Mr Dalgowan, isn't it?'

'It is. Good evening, Mrs Low.'

'I didn't expect to see you in weather like this.'

'It's due to the weather that I'm here,' he told her ruefully. 'I was on my way home when the blizzard made me change my mind and decide to stay the night.'

'Och, now!' she exclaimed, evidently flustered. 'And we don't have a single vacant room. But it would be madness to travel farther on a night like this, so you're more than welcome to a couch in front of the fire and the use of the family bathroom—which is just through the archway on the right—if that will do?'

'That will do fine, thanks.'

'I'd give you our Duggie's room, but he's home for Christmas, and he's brought his girlfriend with him.' With a sigh, she went on, 'Young people these days are so *casual* when it comes to relationships. It wouldn't have done when I was a girl, but Duggie is always telling Charlie and me that we should move with the times, and I expect he's right...but listen to me rattling on... Now, what about the young lady?'

Glancing at her ringless hands, Ross Dalgowan said, 'Miss Richardson has a room booked.'

Mrs Low opened the register and ran an index finger down the entries. 'Richardson…Richardson… Ah, yes, here we are…'

Then, that flustered look returning, she said, 'I'm afraid we owe you an apology, Miss Richardson. Earlier this evening we found we'd made a mistake and the only accommodation we had left was a small family suite on the ground floor. It's comprised of two adjoining rooms and a bathroom. Hastily she added, 'But, as the mistake was ours, we'll be happy to let you have it for the price we quoted you… Have you any luggage?'

'Just an overnight bag.'

Mrs Low glanced at the cavorting teddy bears on the bag Ross Dalgowan was still holding and rightly identified it.

At that precise moment, another stray drop of water trickled down Cathy's cheek, and Ross reached to wipe it away.

Clearly the intimate gesture gave Mrs Low the wrong impression and, with the air of having solved a thorny problem, she suggested, 'Possibly you could share the suite?'

'I really can't ask Miss Richardson to—'

'If there are two rooms I have no objection to—'

They spoke, and stopped, in unison.

'If I show you, you'll no doubt find it easier to decide.' Emerging from behind the desk, Mrs Low led them briskly through a small, inner hallway and opened a door on the right.

'Although there's central heating, I've lit a fire in this bedroom… So much more welcoming on a night like this, don't you think?'

The room she showed them into was warm and cosy in the leaping firelight. Heavy folkweave curtains had been drawn to keep out the night, and a single lamp cast a pool of golden light.

There was a double bed with an old-fashioned patchwork

quilt, a tallboy, a wardrobe, a carved blanket chest and, set in front of the hearth, a low table and two comfortable-looking armchairs.

To one side of the fireplace was a wicker basket of logs and a big pile of fir cones. The aromatic scent of pine resin mingled with lavender hung in the air.

Through a curtained archway was another small room, not much bigger than a large cupboard, with bunk beds and a narrow fitted wardrobe.

Glancing up at Ross Dalgowan's six feet two inches, Mrs Low said doubtfully, 'I'm afraid the bunk beds were only intended for children, but even one of them might be more comfortable, and give you a tidy bit more privacy than a couch. And this is the bathroom…'

Though old-fashioned, the bathroom was spotlessly clean and had every facility, including a walk-in shower cubicle.

'There are plenty of towels and toiletries, even a disposable shaving kit, if you do decide to share.'

Looking from one to the other, she added, 'While you talk it over why don't you sit in front of the fire and get warm? I'll bring you in a nice bite of supper.'

Satisfied that she'd done the best she could, she hurried away.

Putting Cathy's bag on the chest, Ross Dalgowan raised a well-marked brow and asked, 'Do you have any problem with Mrs Low's kindly meant suggestion? If you do…'

Recognizing that it was politeness rather than diffidence that had made him ask, she answered. 'No, no, of course I don't.'

'In that case…' He helped her off with her coat before removing his own and hanging them both on some convenient pegs.

She saw that he was wearing smart-casual trousers and an olive-green jerkin over a toning shirt. His watch looked expensive, and his shoes appeared to be handmade.

Although there was nothing blatant, his whole appearance suggested affluence and power, while his air of ease spoke of a quiet self-assurance.

Taking a mobile phone from his pocket, he said, 'If you'll excuse me just a minute? So they won't worry, I'd like to give the folks who are expecting me a call to say I'll be staying here for the night.'

'Of course.'

While he made the call, she moved to sit by the blazing log fire.

Addressing the person who answered as Marley, he kept it brief and to the point, ending, 'See you tomorrow, then. Bye.'

Cathy found herself wondering if Marley was his wife and rather hoping not, until she pulled herself up short, reminding herself sternly that it was none of her business.

Dropping the phone back into his pocket, Ross joined her in front of the fire, remarking, 'Your shoes look as if they're saturated. Why don't you take them off and warm your feet?'

She had been longing to do just that, and, needing no further encouragement, she slipped them off and, propping them by the fender to dry, held her slim feet out to the blaze.

There was a drifting silence for a minute or so while he stared into the leaping flames and she studied him covertly.

The strong face held a certain aloofness, a touch of arrogance, a hint of sensuality. He was, she guessed, a complex man with many layers.

His mouth, with its ascetic upper lip and passionate lower, was beautiful, and his thick lashes were ridiculously long and curly. Combined with so much sheer masculinity, that mouth and those lashes had a stunning effect, and she felt hollow inside.

He glanced up suddenly, and as she looked anywhere but at him, he queried, 'Warmer now?'

'Much warmer,' she answered abstractedly.

'How long were you on the road?'

Pulling herself together, she told him, 'I left London mid-morning. But though I only stopped briefly for a sandwich and a cup of coffee, it took much longer to reach the border than I'd expected.'

'You're from London?'

'Yes.'

'Where are you heading for?'

'The Cairngorms. A small place called Luing.'

A flicker of something that she couldn't decipher crossed his face, before he said, 'Yes, I know it well. You were right to break the journey. It's quite a distance. I take it you ski?'

'Yes, but not particularly well, I'm sorry to say. Do you?'

'I was born and brought up on the edge of the Cairngorms, so during the winter months I practically lived on skis.'

'I'm afraid my experience has been confined to childhood holidays in the Alps.'

'Sounds fun.'

'Yes, they were.'

Without thinking, she voiced the thought that was in her mind. 'To say you were born in Scotland you don't have much of an accent.'

'My father's family were Scottish born and bred, but my mother was English. When I was fourteen and my sister was eleven our parents divorced, and our mother went to live in London. Though my father and I didn't always see eye to eye, I stayed with him and his second wife until I was eighteen and got a place at Oxford.

'After I'd graduated I moved to London and went into the Information Technology business with a couple of friends. I'd always intended to come back to Scotland eventually, but at the moment I'm still living in London while I tie up some loose ends.'

'Which part of town?'

'I've a flat in Belmont Square.'

The fact that he lived in Mayfair seemed to confirm her first impression that he was well off.

Eager to know more about him, but wary of making the questions too personal, she asked, 'Do you get up to Scotland much?'

'Four or five times a year.'

'For business or pleasure?'

'You could say both.'

There was a tap at the door and Mrs Low came bustling in, a voluminous apron tied at her waist, wheeling a supper trolley.

'Here we are,' she said cheerfully. 'There's a nice drop of my cock-a-leekie, some hot oatcakes wrapped round ham, an apple pie and cream, and I thought a big jug of coffee wouldn't go amiss.'

As she spoke, she wheeled the trolley to where they could comfortably reach, adding, 'I'm afraid it's all very simple...'

'Thanks, Mrs Low,' Ross Dalgowan said. 'As far as I'm concerned, it's a feast. It was very good of you to go to so much trouble.'

Cathy added her agreement and thanks.

Looking pleased, Mrs Low said, 'Whist, now, it was no trouble at all.' Then, beaming at them, she added, 'Oh, and when I told Charlie you were here, he said to leave this with you and advise you and the young lady to have a wee dram or two to keep out the cold.'

Like a conjuror pulling a rabbit out of a hat, from a deep pocket in her apron she produced a bottle of Highland single malt and two whisky glasses wrapped in a white napkin.

'Please give him our thanks.'

'You'll have a word with him before you go?'

'I certainly will.'

She stooped to put fresh logs on the fire before going on, 'The bunk beds are already made up, and I've left a pillow and some blankets on one of the couches in the lounge, so you can decide at your leisure which suits you best.

'Now, if there's nothing else either of you need I'm away to my bed. With a house full of guests I have to be up very early, so I'll say goodnight to you both.'

'Goodnight,' they answered in unison.

At the door, she paused to say, 'I almost forgot to tell you, there'll be breakfast from six-thirty onwards. The breakfast room is just off the lounge… Oh, and when you've finished eating, perhaps you'll put the trolley outside?'

When the door had closed behind her, Ross Dalgowan poured coffee for Cathy and himself, remarking thoughtfully, 'If you only had a sandwich at lunchtime you must be hungry.'

'I am, rather.'

'Then tuck in.'

They enjoyed a leisurely supper without speaking, the only sounds the crackling of the logs and the wind soughing mournfully in the chimney.

As though comfortable with himself, his companion and his surroundings, Ross Dalgowan seemed quite content with the silence, and Cathy was pleased.

Neil, invariably uncomfortable with silence, had needed to fill every second with the sound of his own voice. Convinced he knew everything there was to know, he had talked whenever he had a listener.

But this man was different. He had a maturity Neil would never have and he was, she guessed, much quieter by nature.

She and Neil had first met when she had been a shy, naive

nineteen and he was an experienced twenty, and she had been duly impressed by his strikingly handsome face and his apparent depth of knowledge.

After a whirlwind courtship—although he had been a penniless student—at his insistence they had got married, and he had moved in with her.

He had been about to start his last year at college, and because he had had no family to help she had found herself struggling to pay off his debts and support him, as well as Carl.

Even so, he had complained about her brother living with them, until she had told him firmly that it was, and always had been, Carl's home.

'Oh, very well,' he'd said sulkily. 'I suppose it'll only be until he can get a job and find a place of his own.'

Relieved that he had accepted the situation, she had done her best to make him happy.

It wasn't until they were married that she had discovered how empty and shallow he really was, and that his cleverness and his handsomeness—like the ripples on a pool—were all on the surface.

But, even after such a brief acquaintance, Cathy was already sure that Ross Dalgowan, who was sitting so quietly, was anything but shallow.

Watching him surreptitiously, she noticed that in the heat from the fire his hair had dried to the colour of ripe corn, and it struck her as strange that such a very masculine man should be so fair.

Neil had been blond, but fair-skinned, with pale brows and lashes and almost girlish features.

Whereas this man was tough-looking, with brows and lashes several shades darker than his hair and the kind of skin that would tan easily.

Though Neil had proved to be greedy and selfish and vain—
a narcissist to the core—he'd been a golden boy that the
opposite sex had fawned over.

A woman's darling.

Ross Dalgowan would be a woman's darling, she had little
doubt, but he would also be a man's man, where Neil had had
few, if any, male friends.

When she had first met Neil, he'd appeared to be charming
and easygoing, willing to live and let live. But in reality—
like some weak people—he had been spoilt and peevish, a
bully at heart.

Her companion, she was oddly certain, would be neither
spoilt nor peevish, and while he might be masterful, she
couldn't see him being a bully.

Watching him, she noticed that he ate with a healthy
appetite, but neatly and noiselessly.

Unlike Neil, who, in spite of his somewhat effeminate good
looks and his general air of delicacy, had tended to bolt his food.
Rather like a greedy schoolboy who hadn't yet learned either
manners or self-control.

She had discovered, to her cost, that the same went for his
sexual appetite.

They had been married only a matter of months when, after
drinking too much wine, he'd tried to force himself on her.

Failing, he had lashed out at her, calling her a lot of things,
amongst which 'a frigid bitch' was the kindest by far.

Sighing, she pushed thoughts of the unhappy past aside
and, glancing up, found herself looking into eyes the grey of
woodsmoke—fascinating eyes that tilted up a little at the outer
edge.

Her head whirling, and a strange tingle running along her
nerve ends, she tore her gaze away.

Sensitive to her mood, Ross asked, 'Problems?'

'No, not really.'

Though he obviously didn't believe her, he let the matter drop, and they continued the meal in companionable silence.

'More coffee?' he queried when they had both finished eating.

'No, thank you.'

'Then I'll get rid of this.' He rose to his feet and put the trolley outside.

Returning to his seat, he suggested, 'Suppose we have a "wee dram" before we turn in, as Mrs Low's husband advised?'

Though normally she never drank spirits, wanting to keep him with her a little longer, she agreed, 'Yes, why not?'

He opened the bottle and, having poured a finger of whisky into both glasses, handed her one.

Raising his own glass, he toasted, 'Here's to the future, and our better acquaintance.'

His words, and the look in his eyes, brought a surge of warmth and excitement, and she found herself yearning for something this man seemed to offer. Something poignant. Something magic. Something that would last a lifetime. True love, perhaps…?

Telling herself not to be foolish, she tore her gaze away with an effort and took an incautious sip of her drink. The strong spirit made her cough.

His lips twitched, but, hiding his amusement—if indeed it *was* amusement—he said, 'Just to prove that I've lived in England for a long time, I'll act like a Sassenach and ask if you'd prefer some water with it?'

'Yes, I would,' she answered gratefully, and started to rise to fetch it.

But Ross was already on his feet, and he pressed her gently back into the chair. 'Stay where you are. I'll get it.'

He disappeared into the bathroom and returned after a moment with glass of water. 'Say when.'

When there was about twice as much water as whisky, she said, 'That should be fine, thank you.'

'Try it and see.'

She tried a sip and, breathing a sigh of relief, told him, 'Much better.'

Putting the rest of the water by the whisky bottle, he smiled at her.

His teeth gleamed white and even, and his mouth, with its intriguing hint of controlled passion, made her feel strange inside.

Becoming aware that she had been staring at him, she looked back into the glowing fire. But the cosy familiarity had gone, leaving an awareness, a rising excitement, a sexual tension.

Needing to break the silence and return to the more mundane, she swallowed and, her normally clear voice decidedly husky, asked, 'Are you up here for Christmas, Mr Dalgowan?'

'Yes, and New Year. But won't you call me Ross? It seems ridiculous to stand on ceremony.'

'Of course, if you call me Cathy.'

'How long are you in Scotland for, Cathy?'

Reminded of just *why* she was in Scotland, and flustered by the innocent question, she answered, 'I'm not quite sure... Christmas and New Year...'

'Do you have anyone important in your life? A partner, perhaps?'

Unwilling to talk about her brief and disastrous marriage and the subsequent divorce, she answered briefly, 'No.'

Though they had only just met, and he knew scarcely anything about her, Ross felt a rush of gladness that shook him with its strength and vehemence.

After Lena, he had taken care to avoid any emotional entanglements, keeping the occasional liaison light, casual, a simple, straightforward exchange of pleasure, with no looking back and no regrets when they parted.

Now he found himself doubting that that would be enough with this woman.

He sat quietly watching her, and holding her breath, aware that somehow the answer mattered, she seized the opportunity to ask, 'How about you?'

'No, no one.'

She was breathing a sigh of relief when he added, 'I did have plans to marry earlier this year, but they didn't work out. Though Lena was born in Scotland, and in fact our families lived quite close, she loved the bright lights of London and refused to live anywhere else. Whereas I wanted to live in the country.

'When she couldn't bring me round to her way of thinking, she left me for a wealthy businessman who lives in Park Lane and never leaves London...'

Cathy heard the underlying bitterness in his voice, and knew that his fiancée's defection still hurt.

'Now, if we happen to be in Scotland at the same time, she makes a point of calling to see me when she's visiting her father.'

It smacked of turning the screw, and Cathy frowned, hardly able to believe that any woman could treat him that way.

Seeing her frown, and misinterpreting it, he apologized quickly, 'I'm sorry. Maybe I shouldn't have got on to such a personal topic, but I wondered if you were perhaps travelling up to join someone?'

Instinctively sure that this man was special, she hesitated, momentarily tempted to try and explain about Carl and the deception she had reluctantly agreed to take part in.

Though, as Carl had frequently pointed out since he had first broached the scheme, it was an innocent enough deception and would do no one any harm. And it would only be necessary until he'd been able to prove his worth.

'I have exactly the qualifications the Bowans are looking for,' he had told her, 'but they were adamant that they would only employ a married couple.'

Then with a sigh he had said, 'Everything would have been fine if Katie hadn't walked out on me and we'd got married as planned. But as it is I badly need your help. And honestly, Sis, it won't be too bad. All we need to do is get on with our respective jobs and pretend to be husband and wife.'

However, intrinsically honest, Cathy was far from happy, and had it been anyone other than her beloved younger brother she would have refused point-blank to be a part of it.

As it was—with his life in ruins after the woman he loved had run off with his best friend—Cathy had found it impossible to deny him the chance to do what he'd always wanted to do.

But her heart sank at the thought of trying to explain all that to Ross Dalgowan...

And after promising Carl she wouldn't breath a word to a soul, how could she?

Turning her back on temptation, she shook her head. 'Not really.'

Her companion seemed satisfied, but, far from happy, she felt the colour rise in her cheeks and hoped he would put it down to the heat of the fire.

CHAPTER TWO

Ross helped them both to more whisky, then, taking Cathy by surprise, observed, 'You have the most beautiful and fascinating eyes.'

With a self-deprecating smile, he added, 'But I'm afraid I'm telling you something you already know.'

Cathy had often wished that her eyes were the same deep blue as Carl's, and her voice was a little unsteady as she admitted, 'I've always considered that they were no particular colour, just nondescript.'

'Far from it. Not only are they a lovely shape, but they seem to change colour with the light, as opals do. A moment ago they looked blue, now they look green and gold, like an April day.'

She might have thought he was merely chatting her up, but he spoke quietly, thoughtfully, as if he meant exactly what he said.

Watching her blush deepen, he said contritely, 'But now I've embarrassed you.' Then, smoothly changing tack, he asked, 'Are you London born and bred?'

'No, both my brother and I were born in Kent. We only moved to London when my parents—my father was a doctor and my mother a physiotherapist—got posts at one of the London hospitals.'

'I see. Are either you or your brother in the medical profession?'

'My brother trained as a physiotherapist, and I had hoped to be a doctor.'

Reaching to put a couple of fresh logs on the fire, he probed, 'Hoped to be?'

'I left school just before I was eighteen, when both my parents were killed in a plane crash.'

'You and your brother weren't involved in the crash?'

She shook her head. 'No. To celebrate twenty years together they decided to go on a second honeymoon.' Though she did her best to speak dispassionately, even after almost seven years the sense of loss still showed.

'Is your brother older than you?'

She shook her head. 'No, a year younger.'

'That must have been tough,' he said simply, but his face held compassion, as if he understood.

'It was for a while, but we managed.'

Seeing that talking about it made her sad, he let the subject drop, asking instead, 'Have you been to the Cairngorms before?'

'No, but I've always wanted to. I love mountains.'

'It's a beautiful area,' he agreed, 'but, apart from on the fringes, relatively isolated. There are no roads in the heartland, I'm pleased to say, so it's best seen on foot, on horseback or on skis...'

For a while he talked about Scotland, and his low, pleasant voice, combined with the meal she had just eaten, the warmth and the unaccustomed whisky, made her feel sleepy and contented.

She was just stifling a yawn when he asked, 'Getting tired? If you want me to leave so you can go to bed...?'

Feeling bereft at the thought of him going, she denied, 'No, no...I'm not really tired. It's just the warmth of the fire...'

'Well, when you *do* want me to go, don't hesitate to say so.'

While the logs sparked and crackled and the blizzard raged outside, they talked idly, casually. But beneath the surface an unspoken, yet much deeper kind of communication was taking place.

Eventually, with evident reluctance, Ross rose to his feet, and remarked, 'You've still got a fairly long drive tomorrow, so I really must go and let you get some sleep...'

Since her divorce, hurt and bitterly disillusioned, Cathy had steered clear of men, freezing off any that had shown the slightest desire to get too intimate.

But now the thought of Ross Dalgowan leaving made her heart sink, and she faced the fact that, though she knew virtually nothing about him, she *wanted* him to stay.

Taking a deep breath, she said, 'Oh, but I should feel guilty if you were uncomfortable when there's more room here than I need.'

'There's absolutely no reason for you to feel guilty. Where I sleep really isn't a problem. I've no objection to stretching out on one of the couches in the lounge.'

'They're much too short,' she pointed out a shade breathlessly, 'and you would have no privacy.'

Already he knew that this woman was different, special—not the kind he could lightly walk away from—and, remembering his decision to avoid emotional entanglements, he knew he should go. But very tempted to stay, to see what came of it, he hesitated.

Seeing that hesitation, she went on in a rush, 'The bunk beds don't look particularly inviting, but if you want stay in the suite—which you can do with pleasure—at least you'll be able to shower and take off your clothes.'

'The thought of not having to sleep in my clothes makes your offer practically irresistible,' he told her with a grin.

'Then stay.'

'Well, if you're sure?'

'I'm sure.' To leave no doubt in his mind, she added, 'The bathroom's yours when you want it.'

Shaking his head, he told her, 'Ladies first.'

While Cathy found her toilet bag and night things, he resumed his seat by the fire.

When she had showered, wearing a plastic cap to keep her hair dry, she cleaned her teeth and put on her nightdress.

Looking in the mirror while she removed the pins from her thick coil of fair hair and brushed out the long silken mass, she saw that her cheeks were a little flushed and her eyes were bright, as though something wonderful had happened to her.

Warning herself that she mustn't get carried away, she pulled on her robe, tied the belt and, picking up her pile of clothes, returned to the bedroom.

Just the sight of him made her heart leap.

He was sitting staring into the fire as though lost in thought, the ruddy glow turning his face into the mask of an Inca god.

Putting her clothes beside her bag, she took a deep breath and told him, 'Your turn now.'

He rose, his glance running over her slender figure in the clinging ivory satin. She saw his grey eyes darken to charcoal, then saw the little lick of flame that had nothing to do with the firelight.

For a moment they gazed into each other's eyes, before, turning on his heel abruptly, Ross made his way into the bathroom, and a moment or two later she heard the shower running.

Finding her knees were trembling, she sank down in the chair she had occupied previously, while her thoughts tumbled over one another in a joyous confusion as she went over the events of the evening spent with Ross.

Some kind of magic had taken place, as though they had both been caught in a spell. He felt it, too, she was certain.

Then, like a dark cloud, came the doubts. Perhaps she was wrong, mistaken. She had been mistaken about Neil, about his feelings. After that fiasco, could she—*dared* she—trust her own judgement?

But she was quite a few years older now, and much less naive. And Ross was nothing at all like Neil. Apart from the physical attraction she felt, there was so much about him that drew her— a warmth, a sensitivity, a quiet inner strength, a *reliability*.

She didn't hear him return, but some sixth sense made her glance up to find he was standing only a few feet away quietly watching her.

He was freshly shaven, his corn-coloured hair was still slightly damp and trying to curl, and he was wearing one of the navy-blue towelling robes that had been hanging behind the bathroom door.

'Are you sure you're happy about a perfect stranger sharing your suite?' he asked.

Looking up at him, she spoke the exact truth. 'You don't seem like a stranger. I know it sounds incredible, but I feel as if I've always known you.'

He took a step forward, and stooped to brush a strand of hair back from her cheek.

She caught her breath.

His hands closing lightly around her upper arms, he lifted her to her feet. Gazing down at her, he said softly, 'Yes, I was sure you felt the same rapport, the same sense of closeness. It was there when I looked in your eyes.

'But though I'm certain we have something special going for us, it's early days yet, so if you want me to use one of bunk beds...?'

She didn't. But, too shy to say so outright, she bent her head and mumbled, 'What do *you* want?'

He lifted her chin and studied her face.

A couple of hours in her company had confirmed his first impression that she was the loveliest thing he'd ever seen.

There was no trace of hardness or worldliness about her; instead mingled with a faint aura of sadness was a certain innocence, a sweetness, a vulnerability that touched his heart.

His voice a little husky, he said, 'You can't possibly not know. I want to hold you, to kiss you, to feel your naked body against mine. I want to take you to bed and make love to you until we're both up there with the stars, then I want to sleep with you in my arms.'

All her life she'd been cautious, inhibited, and after her disastrous relationship with Neil she'd felt frozen through and through, certain she'd never feel the warmth of true love, the pleasure of being held in caring arms.

Now, however, her inhibitions gone—driven away by the unaccustomed whisky, perhaps?—she longed to reach out and take the happiness that this man seemed to be offering.

But suppose she was frigid, as Neil had charged?

Ross had been watching her face, the changing expressions, and now, with a slight sigh, he released her arms and stepped back.

His voice level, he told her, 'Don't worry, I'll take the couch...'

He was turning to walk away when she whispered, 'Don't go. Please, don't go.'

'I think I'd better.' Wryly he added, 'It might prove too much of a temptation if I slept on one of the bunks.'

'But I don't want you to sleep in the other room.'

'Are you sure? A moment ago you looked seriously worried at the thought of me sharing your bed.'

'No, no… It wasn't that,' she said. 'But I…I don't usually behave like this.'

'I never thought you did. But, as I said, it's early days yet, so if you're not happy…'

'I am happy,' she assured him. 'Please stay.'

With a little inarticulate murmur he rested his forehead against hers, melting her heart with the tenderness of the gesture, and bringing unexpected tears to her eyes.

As he lifted his head, twin teardrops escaped and trickled down her cheeks.

He kissed them away softly, before touching his lips to hers.

She was still trembling from the delight of that kiss when he drew her close and kissed her again.

Contact with his firm, muscular body turned her very bones to jelly, and she melted against him, her lips parting helplessly beneath the light, yet masterful pressure of his.

With a little murmur of satisfaction he deepened the kiss while he unfastened her robe and slipped it off her shoulders, letting it puddle at her feet.

As he kissed her, his hands moved over her seductively, tracing her slender hips and buttocks through the thin satin of her nightdress before moving up again to the soft curve of her breasts.

Feeling her body's instinctive response, he cupped the weight of one breast in the palm of his hand and rubbed his thumb over the firming nipple.

He heard her soft gasp, and, slipping the satin straps from her shoulders, he sent the nightdress to join the robe at their feet. Then, taking one pink, velvety nipple in his mouth, he teased its fellow between his finger and thumb.

For a while, with a skill and delicacy that Neil had totally lacked, he pleasured her, before pulling back the covers and lifting her onto the bed.

He was standing looking down at her, admiring her flawless skin, the firm, beautifully shaped breasts, the enticing flare of her hips, and the long, slender legs, when she opened dazed eyes.

Smiling down at her, he discarded the towelling robe, switched off the bedside lamp, and, stretching out beside her, with hands and mouth he explored her body, finding every erogenous zone and producing the most exquisite sensations, the kind of singing pleasure she had never known before.

He whispered softly how beautiful she was, how desirable, how much her body delighted him, while he brought her to a fever pitch of wanting.

Just for an instant when he moved over her she felt a touch of panic. Suppose she couldn't respond? Suppose he was disappointed?

But as though sensing her fear, he kissed her gently, reassuringly, and the panic died.

Then in the flickering firelight, while the blizzard beat at the window panes with frozen fingers, he made love to her, tenderly, passionately, so that she was caught up and carried along by the wonder of it.

Never in her wildest dreams had she imagined love could be like this, and after a climax of such intensity that she thought she might die, she slowly drifted back to earth to lie in a blissful haze.

After a while, her breathing and heart-rate returned to something approaching normal, and she became aware that his fair head was pillowed on her breast.

She lay quietly, savouring the pleasure of it, until he stirred and lifted himself away.

At this point Neil had invariably turned his back, leaving her cold and unsatisfied, with a leaden feeling of depression, of failure, as though the fault was hers.

And though this time she was warm and satisfied, the remembrance of that failure was descending like a fog when Ross leaned over her and, taking his weight on his elbows, kissed her mouth deeply, tenderly.

Then, his lips wandering over her face and throat, punctuating the words with soft, baby kisses, he told her how infinitely desirable she was, how warm and responsive, and how much he had enjoyed making love to her.

His words and his kisses dispersed the miasma as sunlight dispersed mist, and, her heart light, her spirits rising, for the first time in her adult life she felt happy, fulfilled, like a real woman.

He turned on his back, and, as though he didn't want to lose contact, he gathered her to him and, his body half supporting hers, settled her head on the comfortable juncture between chest and shoulder.

She lay contentedly, enjoying the strong beat of his heart beneath her cheek, the feel of his skin against hers, the clean male smell of him and the scent of his aftershave.

Never in her wildest imaginings could she have visualized all her dreams coming true like this. To have an unspoken longing, a tenuous hope, a hidden desire become wonderful reality so fast seemed almost unbelievable.

He was everything she had ever wanted in a man, and she thanked fate for the snowfall that had brought him into her life.

Though she wanted to stay awake for a while to savour the magic of it all, in the blink of an eye she was asleep—deeply, dreamlessly.

Some time during the night Ross awakened her with a kiss and a soft caress, and they made love again.

For Cathy it was a rocket trip to the stars, and when it was over she lay in his arms, blissfully happy, and once more thanked fate for bringing him into her life.

Her last thought before sleep claimed her once more was that now their instant and mutual attraction had become so serious so quickly, over breakfast she must explain about Carl and the deception she'd agreed to.

She could always ask him to keep it to himself until Carl had managed to prove his worth and was able to tell his employers the truth…

In the early hours of the morning she started to dream. She was lying contentedly in bed in the arms of her lover, while they made wonderful plans for their future together.

Then in her dream she heard the urgent shrill of a phone, and, summoned away, her lover left her side.

Cold and bereft, she wept soundlessly, heartbroken, until he returned and she felt the brush of his lips as he kissed her softly.

But it was a goodbye kiss.

She put her arms around his neck and tried to keep him, to make him stay, but as though she was embracing a wraith he slipped from her grasp and walked away, and in the way that dreamers do she knew he was gone for ever.

Still, she searched for him everywhere, through strange, empty rooms and on every busy street, scanning faces as they went past, and in despair stopping anyone who looked remotely like him.

Then she saw him walking just ahead of her and, filled with joy, she ran after him and caught his arm. But when he turned to face her it was Neil and, his eyes cold and uncaring, he pulled his arm free and pushed her roughly away.

Though the disturbing dreams went on, they grew vague, hazy, until eventually she fell into a more settled slumber.

From then on she slept deeply, until her brain finally stirred into life and struggled to free itself from the clinging cobwebs of sleep.

But even when she was almost awake, she was aware of a lingering feeling of sadness and loss.

Opening her eyes, she found herself in a strange room. It was a split second before memory kicked in, and she recalled everything that had happened the previous night. The unexpected snow, meeting Ross, the instant attraction that had flared between them and the delight and magic they had shared.

Her spirits soaring, a smile on her lips, she turned towards him.

But the place beside her was cold and empty. If she smoothed the sheets and plumped up the pillow the last traces of him would be gone and it would be hard to believe he had even existed.

Pushing the gloomy thought away, she glanced at her watch. Almost eight-thirty.

He was probably shaving.

She clambered out of bed and, pulling on her robe, headed for the bathroom. But even before she tapped on the door the utter stillness convinced her that he wasn't there.

When she opened the door, the two towelling robes hanging side by side and the absence of his clothes confirmed the fact that he was gone.

He must be having breakfast.

But why hadn't he awakened her so they could breakfast together?

Her heart grew cold.

Had she been mistaken after all? Had Ross—despite his caring words—seen her simply as a one-night stand? A casual bed partner that he felt nothing for?

Turning away, she saw the note on the floor—a small, flimsy page torn from a pocket diary and almost hidden by the quilt. It must have fluttered off the bedside cabinet.

She picked it up with a hand that wasn't quite steady.

Though obviously hurried, the writing was firm and decisive. It said simply:

> You were sleeping so soundly it seemed a shame to waken you. Thank you for last night. You were a delight. Mrs Low will explain why I'm having to rush off. Have a safe journey up to Luing, and I'll see you as soon as I possibly can. Ross.

She hadn't told him exactly where she was staying, so unless Luing was a very small place how would he find her? She desperately wanted him to. But if he turned up asking for a *Miss* Richardson, it could cause problems. Oh, if only she had explained about Carl...

But perhaps he hadn't gone yet. She might be in time to catch him...

She showered quickly, brushed her hair and coiled it neatly, then, having put on fresh undies and the fine wool suit she'd worn the previous day, she hurried along to the breakfast room.

But it was empty apart from an elderly couple who were just on the point of leaving.

As they exchanged a civil good morning, Mrs Low came busily in.

'Ah, there you are, Miss Richardson,' she exclaimed. 'Perfect timing. Mr Dalgowan said if you weren't down for breakfast by nine o'clock I was to call you.'

'Has he gone?'

'Oh, yes, he left before five-thirty. I was barely up myself. I understand he'd had a phone call from home in the early hours of the morning to say there was some kind of emergency...'

It must have been the phone ringing that had started her off dreaming, Cathy realized, and sighed. If only she had awakened properly and been able to talk to him before he left.

But Mrs Low was going on. 'The poor man didn't even stop for a bite to eat, he just swallowed a cup of coffee and went, saying he'd be sure to see you as soon as may be. Luckily a warm front followed the blizzard through, so instead of freezing the snow has turned to slush, which means the main roads should be clear.

'Now, what would you like for breakfast? We've bacon and eggs, or a pair of nice kippers?'

A mixture of excitement and apprehension over what the day might bring robbing her of her appetite, she said, 'Just coffee, please.'

'Well, if you're sure?'

'Quite sure, thanks.'

When Mrs Low had gone, Cathy walked to the window and looked out.

Though the garden was still mostly covered with white there were several dark patches where the snow had already gone, and the trees and bushes were bare and dripping.

As Mrs Low had said, the main roads should be clear, so Ross would be well on his way home by now. But where was home?

Though he'd talked about being born on the edge of the Cairngorms and had said he knew Luing well, he hadn't told her exactly where he lived. So there was no way she could get in touch with him.

Once again she wished fervently that she had explained about Carl. But she hadn't. And now it was too late.

When her coffee arrived, Cathy said, 'I'd like to make a start as soon as possible, so if you can let me have the bill?'

'Mr Dalgowan took care of that,' Mrs Low told her. 'He's a fine young man, good-looking and generous to a fault...'

'How well do you know him?' Cathy asked.

'He stayed here in the autumn when his car broke down. Charlie and he got talking and discovered they had some mutual friends. He promised to call in and see us next time he was passing.'

'Do you know exactly where he lives?'

Looking somewhat surprised at the question, Mrs Low answered vaguely, 'The name of his house just escapes me, but it's on the edge of the Cairngorms, a few miles from Luing, I believe...

'Oh, excuse me, I think I hear the phone ringing. In case I'm not around when you leave, I'll say goodbye now. Have a safe journey...' She hurried away and a moment later the ringing stopped.

As soon as Cathy had drunk her coffee, she went along to her room and packed her night things and toilet bag, before taking the ring she would need to wear from her handbag.

It was her mother's wedding ring—Neil had taken Cathy's when he'd left, along with everything else he could lay his hands on. Because of the distinctive engraving it had been amongst the pitifully few belongings that had been returned to Cathy and Carl after the plane crash.

Slipping the wide gold band chased with lover's knots onto the third finger of her left hand, she discovered it was quite loose. Which meant she must be careful not to lose it before she could find some way to make it a better fit.

With a sigh, and one last look around the room that held such happy memories, she pulled on her coat and hurried out to the four-wheel drive.

Though the damp air felt chill, the snow had melted and slid off the roof and windscreen, and a watery sun was trying to shine. She stowed away her bag, climbed into the car and started the engine.

The drive was still slushy, and the car slid a little on the humpback bridge, but as soon as Cathy reached the main entrance she found the road was clear in either direction.

It proved, in many ways, to be an enjoyable journey. She was making reasonably good time and the scenery en route was picturesque.

Towards lunchtime she looked for somewhere to have a sandwich and a hot drink, but, unable to find anywhere suitable, she pressed on.

Then just north of Blair Brechan she took the wrong road, and it was late afternoon when, with fresh snow falling, she neared her destination.

Luing turned out to be a tiny hamlet with a backdrop of wonderful scenery. It was made up of a hill farm, five whitewashed cottages and an old grey kirk huddled together at the junction where three narrow roads converged.

The rotting remains of what had obviously once been a signpost lay forlornly on its side, one arm in the air and partially covered by snow.

Uncertain which road to take, Cathy was hesitating when a man wearing a heavy mac and a deerstalker appeared with a spaniel at his heels.

Rolling down the window, she called, 'I wonder if you can help me. I'm looking for Beinn Mor.'

'You'll be wanting the road straight ahead, lassie, and it's a mile or so farther on.'

She thanked him gratefully and set off on the final lap of her journey.

On her left the road—little more than a lane—was edged

with pine trees, and soon on her right an old stone wall came into view and began to meander alongside the road.

After about a mile and a half she came to a pair of massive stone gateposts topped with snarling lions that seemed to forbid entrance. In contrast, the black wrought-iron gates were drawn back, open wide in welcome.

Alongside the entrance a dark green board with gold writing announced that she had reached Dunbar Estate and the Beinn Mor Hotel and Ski Lodge.

Snow was falling softly, gently drifting down as if it were in no particular hurry, as she drove up the winding drive. It was starting to get dark, and the long, low building that came into view was a blaze of lights.

Though she had been warned that the Scots celebrated New Year more than Christmas, it was a lovely Christmassy scene that met her eyes.

Yule tide lanterns on long poles had been placed at intervals, swags of greenery adorned the porch, and a tall, beautifully decorated Christmas tree stood in a massive pot to one side of the entrance.

When she drew up on the forecourt, the heavy oak door opened and Carl—who had obviously been watching for her—appeared, a tall, slim woman with blonde hair by his side.

As Cathy got out into the cold, crisp air that smelt of frost, he hurried over.

For the first time since Katie had left him he looked excited and happy, and, despite the difficulties she knew lay ahead, Cathy rejoiced at the sight of him.

'Darling, it's great to see you.' He gave her a hug and, his lips close to her ear, whispered, 'Everything's going wonderfully well. I hope you remembered the ring?'

'Yes, I'm wearing it,' she whispered back.

Giving her another grateful hug, he said in his normal voice, 'Come and meet Mrs Bowan... I'll do the unpacking later.'

An arm around her, he escorted her to where the blonde woman waited beneath the shelter of the porch.

At close quarters Cathy could see that, though she wasn't strictly speaking beautiful, she was very attractive, with good features, light blue eyes and naturally blonde hair. She was also much younger than Cathy had expected.

Carl introduced the two of them. 'Darling, I'd like you to meet Mrs Bowan... Margaret, this is my wife, Cathy.'

'It's very nice to meet you...Cathy.' Then, with an apologetic smile, Margaret added, 'I'm so sorry, but I'd got it into my head that your name was Katie.'

So, at some time, no doubt during his first interview and before the break-up, Carl must have mentioned that his future wife was called Katie.

Feeling horribly guilty that she was deceiving this nice, friendly-looking woman, Cathy murmured, 'How do you do, Mrs Bowan?'

'Oh, call me Margaret, please. We don't stand on ceremony here. Now, come on in out of the cold and we'll have a nice cup of tea before Carl takes you over to your flat.'

Pushing open the door, on which a holly wreath entwined with scarlet ribbons hung, she ushered them into a warm, nicely decorated lobby-cum-lounge.

Two soft leather couches, several armchairs and a couple of low tables were grouped in front of the blazing fire.

On the left at the far end was a semicircular bar with a scattering of high stools, and on the right a polished reception desk.

Behind the desk, going through a sheaf of papers, was a pretty young woman with dark curly hair.

'This is Janet Muir,' Margaret said. 'She helps to run the place. I don't know what I'd do without her… Janet, this is Cathy, Carl's wife…'

Once again Cathy cringed inwardly, but, murmuring an acknowledgement to the friendly greeting, she returned Janet's smile.

'Have you time to join us for a cup of tea?' Margaret asked the other woman.

Janet shook her head. 'Thanks, but I'd better finish what I'm doing.'

Opening a door to the right that said 'Private', Margaret led the way into a small but cosy room where a teatray had been set on a low table in front of the hearth.

'This is our sitting room, and through there is our bedroom, a bathroom and a small kitchen. As you can guess, it's a bit cramped.

'My brother, who owns the Dunbar Estate, would be only too happy for us to live in the main house, but when the lodge and the log cabins are full, as they are at the moment, we feel that we need to be here on the spot, just in case there are any problems. Do take your coat off and sit down.'

Waving them to a couch in front of a cheerful fire, she sat down opposite and smiled at them both, before asking, 'So what kind of journey did you have?'

Her mouth so dry with nerves that she could hardly speak, Cathy managed, 'It was very good on the whole. Though I was rather surprised to run into snow quite so soon.'

Reaching to pour the tea, Margaret said, 'Yes, we've had several quite heavy falls already this season, which of course is good for the skiing, if not for travelling… Sugar?'

'No, thank you.'

When she had handed them a cup of tea each, she offered a

plate of homemade cake. 'Janet makes the best fruitcake you've ever tasted.'

Unsure whether she could swallow it, Cathy declined, but, with an appreciative murmur, Carl accepted a piece.

'You don't know what you're missing, S—' On the verge of saying *Sis*, he pulled himself up short and changed it to, 'Sweetheart'.

'It certainly smells delicious,' Cathy said and, wishing she was anywhere but where she was, added, 'But I'm not really hungry.'

Margaret smiled at her. 'In that case, as we're all invited to have dinner at Dunbar tonight, it would make sense not to risk spoiling your meal.'

Then in a heartfelt voice she added, 'We're so pleased and relieved to get a nice married couple like you. Last season was an absolute nightmare. Unfortunately, André, the ski instructor we hired, proved to be a real Casanova. We had several complaints from women, and one from an irate husband, who found André and his wife together in one of the ski huts. She swore that André had lured her there, and her husband threatened us with legal action.'

Refilling their cups, she went on, 'We decided there and then that in the future we would only consider a married couple. So earlier this year, before the season started, we took on a couple who *said* they were married and gave their names as Mr and Mrs Fray. But we soon discovered that they weren't married at all, and each considered themselves free to roam, so we felt justified in asking them to leave...'

Her face burning, Cathy didn't know where to look. This was proving even worse than she had imagined.

CHAPTER THREE

'OF COURSE,' Margaret went on, 'the skiing proper is just getting underway, but so far things seem to be going reasonably well. Though we had something of a scare last night when a couple out on a day's cross-country skiing went missing. Thank the Lord they were eventually found safe and sound...

'But here I am keeping you when you're probably dying to be alone... Your flat is over at the main house. Carl has already settled in, so hopefully it should soon start to feel like home.

'There'll be pre-dinner drinks in the study at seven, which should give you just about enough time to unpack and get settled in.'

Only too anxious to go, Cathy rose to her feet and, with a murmur of thanks for the tea, pulled on her coat and headed for the door, followed by Carl.

Feeling mean and despicable, she wished heartily that she had never agreed to this deception.

But if she hadn't come up to Scotland she would never have met Ross Dalgowan. And meeting him meant more to her than she could say. Just those few hours they had spent together had changed her life and given her a bright and shining hope for the future.

This time the foyer was empty and, as they reached the

porch door and went out into the falling snow, Carl muttered, 'I'm sorry, Sis. I could tell you were loathing every minute.'

'I just feel so bad about it,' Cathy said helplessly. 'She's such a nice woman and I hate having to deceive her.'

'I don't like it any more than you do,' Carl assured her as they made their way to the car, which was already covered with snow. 'But, having once started, we've just got to carry it through... Now, you jump in, and I'll drive.'

Having helped Cathy in and slammed the door, he cleared snow from the wing mirrors before sliding into the driver's seat.

Reaching to fasten his seat belt, and noticing her unhappy face, he begged quietly, 'Please, Sis, this chance means so much to me. I know already that the job is exactly what I've been hoping for, and if it wasn't for having to deceive people I like, I'd be on top of the world...

'Believe me, as soon as they've got to know me, and I've proved that I can do the job and that I'm no Casanova, I'll be more than happy to tell them the truth.'

'Suppose when you do they're so angry at the way you deceived them that they tell you to leave?'

'Having come this far, that's a chance I've got to take. I hope they won't. I already love it here. But if they do then we'll get other jobs, find somewhere else to live. Until then, I'm relying on you to support me.'

With a sigh, she told him, 'Very well, I'll do my best, but I'm no good at living a lie.'

'Neither am I, really,' he said as the engine sprang into life. 'I nearly gave the game away just now by calling you Sis...'

The wipers pushing aside the accumulated snow, and their lights making a golden tunnel through the white, they set off up a steady incline, the four-wheel drive coping well with the loose snow.

'But once we're over this initial period of meeting people and settling in,' he went on, 'and we're both doing the jobs we came here to do, it should prove to be a great deal easier.'

She could only hope so, Cathy thought and, in an effort to drop the uncomfortable subject, asked, 'How far is it to the big house?'

'Dunbar itself is about a mile up the drive, but if you're on foot and go out the back way there's a shortcut through the coppice that only takes a matter of minutes.'

As they reached the top of the rise and turned a corner to begin their descent, Cathy saw lights gleaming through the trees.

In her mind's eye she had formed a picture of 'the big house' as being grey and square and dour, stark and uncompromising in its ugliness.

She couldn't have been more wrong.

Through the dusk and the falling snowflakes she could just make out an old grey house cradled lovingly in a snowy fold of the hills.

Long and low, it had a hotchpotch of crooked chimneys and gable ends, mullioned windows and creeper-covered walls.

It was picturesque and beautiful, and, staring at it, entranced, Cathy murmured, 'My house.'

'What?' Carl asked, startled.

'The house,' she explained. 'Seeing it in the falling snow like this reminded me of a house I once saw in an old paperweight snowstorm.'

The snowstorm had charmed and captivated her, and now she felt the same kind of enchantment as they approached the house and drew up near a side entrance with a glowing lantern over the doorway.

Carl jumped out and, having taken one of Cathy's bigger suitcases from the boot, handed her her overnight bag.

Then fishing in his pocket, he produced a keyring with three

Yale keys on it and proceeded to unlock the door, which opened into a hall with a stone fireplace and a stone-slabbed floor, smoothly polished by many feet.

'At one time this was the servants' hall. But these days there's only a handful of staff to run things.'

Though no fire burnt in the huge grate, it was anything but cold, and when Cathy remarked on the fact, Carl explained that the entire house had discreet central heating.

There were several doors leading off, and, opening the nearest one, he remarked, 'Oh, while I think about it, this door doesn't always close properly. Odd times the latch fails to click into place…'

He led the way into their ground-floor flat and, switching on the lights, went on, 'By the way, we'll be quite private. Even the maid doesn't come in to clean unless she's specifically asked to. So it means that no one is going to know we have separate rooms.'

Cathy, who had been wondering about that, gave an inward sigh of relief.

'Mrs Fife, the housekeeper, got everything ready before I moved in—she even stocked the fridge and the freezer. When I thanked her, she mentioned that if there's anything else you need to go straight to her. She's known to be something of a dragon, but I've managed to charm her.'

'I dare say it was your natural modesty that appealed to her.'

He grinned. 'Come on, I'll show you round before I unpack the rest of our stuff…'

The flat, she found, was spacious and attractive, with long, leaded windows, white walls, black beams and polished oak floorboards.

There was a pleasant living room with modern, comfortable-looking furniture, a well-equipped kitchen with a back door that led out to a small snow-covered patio, and two en suite bedrooms—the first of which Carl was already occupying.

Carrying her case into the second, he went on, 'Incidentally, we both have a set of keys—one for the door we came in by and two for the flat itself. You'll find your set on your dressing table...'

When Cathy had had a chance to look around, he asked a shade anxiously, 'So, what do you think?'

Knowing how much he wanted her to like it, she tried hard to sound enthusiastic as she told him, 'It's very nice. A lot nicer than I'd expected.'

'I hoped you'd be happy here.' Looking vastly relieved, he went to finish emptying the car.

While she unpacked and put her clothes in the wardrobe and chest of drawers, Cathy sighed. She *could* have been happy in this lovely old house, but the fact that she and Carl were here under false pretences took all the pleasure out of it.

At ten minutes to seven, freshly showered and dressed in a plain navy-blue sheath that clung lovingly to her slender curves, evening sandals and pearl drops in her neat lobes, Cathy emerged from her bedroom to find Carl was ready and waiting for her.

Widening her eyes, she commented, 'My, but don't you look fine!'

Darkly handsome in a dinner jacket and black bow tie, he grinned at her. 'I must say, you don't look so bad yourself.'

'Gee, thanks.'

'I could rephrase that if you like and tell you you look gorgeous.'

'Don't bother,' she told him quizzically. 'I've no doubt your first comment was a lot nearer the mark... By the way,' she went on, as he closed the door of the flat behind them, 'I've been meaning to ask you, what's Mrs Bowan's brother like?'

'I haven't met him, but Margaret's told me a lot about him. I gather he's a businessman who at the moment spends most of his time either in London or travelling...'

As they headed for the study, he went on, 'Two or three years ago, when his father died, he inherited the whole of the Dunbar Estate along with a title he never uses. To help Dunbar pay its way, he decided to have some log cabins built and to turn Beinn Mor into a holiday complex in summer and a ski lodge in winter.' Reaching the end of a broad corridor, they went through a stone archway into a baronial-type hall with panelled walls, chandeliers, a huge stone fireplace and a graceful dark oak staircase curving up to a minstrels' gallery.

'This is the main hall,' he told her, 'and just through here is the library-cum-study-cum-office.'

Carl opened one of a pair of double doors and ushered her into a handsome book-lined room with a burgundy carpet and heavy velvet curtains that had been drawn against the night.

Several soft leather armchairs, a couch and an oval coffee table had been grouped in front of a blazing log fire, and to one side a drinks trolley held an assortment of bottles and decanters and crystal glasses.

In front of the windows was a long desk with a state-of-the-art computer and printer and all the latest office equipment. At right angles to it was a smaller desk, kept clear except for a laptop. Each had a leather chair.

The man who stepped forward to greet them was tall and sturdily built, with a pleasant, open face, brown hair, already thinning a little on top, and bright hazel eyes. He looked to be in his late thirties.

Holding out his hand, he introduced himself. 'I'm Robert Munro, the estate manager. You must be Carl?'

As the two men shook hands, Carl said, 'That's right, and this is my wife, Cathy.'

'It's nice to meet you both,' Robert said with grave courtesy.

Liking him on sight, Cathy held out her hand with a smile and a murmured greeting.

At that moment a door at the other end of the room opened and a little group of people came in.

Janet and Margaret, chatting cheerfully together, were accompanied by a dark-haired, good-looking man of medium height who shook hands with Cathy and introduced himself as Kevin Bowan.

The last man through the door was frowning a little abstractedly as he talked into a mobile phone. He was tall and broad-shouldered, with blond hair, strong, clear-cut features and level brows.

The shock was like walking slap into a plate glass window, sending Cathy mentally reeling. All she could do was gape at him as, with a murmured apology, he dropped the phone into his jacket pocket and turned to greet his guests.

When he caught sight of Cathy, his face lit up with surprise and gladness. But the gladness died away as Margaret made the introductions.

'This is Ross Dalgowan, my brother... Ross, I'd like you to meet Carl Richardson. Carl is our new ski instructor and physiotherapist...'

As the two men shook hands, Margaret went on, 'And this is Carl's wife, Cathy, who'll be helping with the office work.'

Wanting desperately to run and hide, but unable to move, Cathy stood rooted to the spot.

Ross's eyes rested for a moment on the wide gold wedding

band she was wearing, before her nerveless fingers were taken in a firm clasp and, with a little nod, he acknowledged smoothly, '*Mrs* Richardson...'

No one appeared to notice the emphasis except Cathy, who flinched inwardly.

Those eyes, the blue-grey of woodsmoke, eyes that had smiled into hers so warmly, now held a look of distaste, an icy contempt that chilled her very soul.

Turning to the drinks trolley, Ross assumed the role of suave host. 'Now, what would you like?'

As she shook her head, her empty stomach churning, he pressed, 'A gin and tonic? Or a sherry, perhaps?'

It seemed easier to accept a sherry than argue.

'Cream or dry?'

'Dry, please.'

'Janet?'

'I'll have the same, please.'

He handed both women a glass of pale amber sherry before turning to his sister and enquiring, 'What about you, Marley?'

'A gin and tonic for me, thanks.'

While he served the rest of the drinks, the talk became general. If someone spoke directly to her, Cathy made an effort to answer, but apart from that, her brain still reeling, she took little or no part in the conversation.

She could only be pleased when they finally went through to the dining room—an attractive panelled room where a refectory table had been set with fine linen, sparkling crystal and silver candelabra.

Finding that Carl was seated on one side of her and Margaret on the other, she breathed a sigh of relief. Her relief was short-lived, however, when she found herself sitting directly opposite Ross.

She longed to make some excuse and leave, but for Carl's sake she had to stick it out.

The meal was very nicely served by a young uniformed maid who, Margaret told her, was 'old Hector's great-granddaughter'.

All three courses looked delicious, and at Margaret's kindly meant urging Cathy accepted a little of each.

But, her mouth dry, her throat tight, and only too aware that Ross's cold gaze seldom left her face, she could hardly manage to swallow a morsel.

So her lack of appetite wouldn't be too obvious, her head bent, her eyes cast down, she silently pushed the food around her plate and made a pretence of eating.

Ross, too, had little to say, leaving it to Margaret and the rest to keep the conversational ball rolling.

For a while the talk was general, then it turned to the blizzard and the missing skiers.

'As you know, I've been away in Rothmier visiting my mother,' Robert said, 'and I only got back a short time ago, so this is the first I've heard of it.'

Margaret took up the tale. 'Well, very late last night we discovered that a middle-aged couple who had gone cross-country skiing hadn't returned, and, of course, there was a blizzard blowing. There was nothing we could do just then, but at about five o'clock this morning we got in touch with Ross, who promised to get home as soon as possible.

'In the meantime, as soon as it was light, Kevin took a search party out. But there was no sign of the couple in the direction they had intended to take.

'I don't need to tell you that Kevin knows the area well, but Ross was born and brought up here and he knows it like the palm of his hand. So as soon as he arrived home he led a second search party and eventually found the couple safe.

'Caught in the blizzard, they'd lost their way and been forced to take what shelter they could in one of the old hunting hides. They were well equipped, and luckily a slightly warmer front had followed the blizzard through, so apart from being very cold and hungry they'd come to no real harm, thank the Lord.'

'It was a blessing they were safe,' Robert agreed, and after a moment the conversation became general once more.

When the meal was over, coffee was served in front of a blazing fire, where two curved corner-unit settees, a long, low coffee table and a couple of easy chairs were grouped around a wide stone hearth.

Hoping to escape attention, Cathy had chosen a seat on one of the corner units when, to her dismay, Ross contrived to sit next to her, so close that their knees were almost touching.

'How long have you been married, Mrs Richardson?' he asked silkily.

Forced to answer such a direct question, she avoided meeting his eyes, which she knew quite well were fixed on her face, and stammered, 'N-not very long, actually.'

As if he'd willed her to look at him, she glanced up, and he met and held her gaze. 'How long is *not very long*?'

Her wits totally scattered, she mumbled, 'Three or four weeks.'

He lifted a level brow. 'If I might say so, you appear rather unsure.'

Tearing her eyes away, she struggled to make a calculation based on the date Carl and Katie *should* have got married. 'It's four weeks today.'

'So you were married on a Friday?'

'Yes,' she agreed, then bit her lip, only too aware that she had sounded uncertain.

'Once again you don't seem particularly sure of your facts.'

Knowing he was deliberately needling her, she pulled herself together and said as levelly as possible, 'I'm quite sure.'

'And you don't regard getting married on a Friday as unlucky?'

'No.'

'A lot of people would.'

When she made no attempt to answer, he pursued, 'Tell me, Mrs Richardson, did you have a church wedding? Or were you married in a register office?'

On slightly firmer ground, she answered, 'In a register office.'

'Oh? Which one?'

The ground cut neatly from under her, she echoed, 'Which one?'

'Yes. Which one?'

Unable to think, she told him where she and Neil had been married and hoped desperately that he would stop this interrogation and leave her alone.

But, as if he knew exactly how she felt and was enjoying her discomfort, he persisted, 'You live in London, I gather?'

'Yes.'

'Whereabouts, exactly?'

Putting her coffee cup down so unsteadily that it rattled in the saucer, she told him, 'Notting Hill.' Then, seeing the next question coming, she added, 'We rented a furnished flat in Oldes Court.'

With a wolfish smile, he said, 'When you say "we" I presume you mean yourself and your husband?'

'Of course.'

'Were you both living there before your marriage?'

'Yes.'

'Have you kept it on?'

'No.'

'Why not?'

'As we expected to be living in Scotland, there was no point.'

He fell silent, and, thinking the ordeal was over, she breathed a sigh of relief.

Prematurely, as it turned out.

Those cold grey eyes pinning her, he asked, 'Where did you go for your honeymoon, Mrs Richardson?'

Glancing at Carl for support, Cathy found he was in earnest conversation with Janet.

'You seem very nervous,' Ross commented.

'There's no wonder she's nervous.' Margaret came to Cathy's aid. 'From the bits of conversation I've overheard, it sounds as if you're giving her the third degree. But there's really no need. I'm quite satisfied that Cathy and Carl really *are* married, unlike our "Mr and Mrs Fray"... And for heaven's sake, Ross,' she added with a look of fond exasperation, 'do stop calling the poor girl Mrs Richardson. Her name's Cathy.'

He smiled sardonically. 'She may not want me to be too familiar.'

'Rubbish. You know perfectly well we're all on first-name terms.'

'Well, if you don't mind...Cathy?'

Taking a deep breath, Cathy said, 'Of course not.'

As Kevin claimed his wife's attention, Ross's inimical gaze returned to Cathy's face. 'Now, where were we? Oh, yes, you were about to tell me where you went on your honeymoon.'

'We didn't have a honeymoon.'

'Any particular reason?'

'With Carl about to start a new job, we decided not to bother.'

'"We decided not to bother" makes me think you're not particularly romantic.'

Catching the last few words, Carl said with a grin, 'That's where you're wrong. Though Cathy's very practical in most ways, she's got a romantic streak a mile wide, and always has had.'

'You sound as if you've known her all your life.'

'I have...pretty well,' Carl added hastily.

Ross's lips twisted in the caricature of a smile. 'So it was a boy and girl romance that finally blossomed into true love?'

Taking the remark at face value, Carl agreed, 'That about sums it up.'

Knowing she couldn't take any more, Cathy got to her feet and, looking at no one in particular, said, 'If you'll excuse me I'm feeling tired and headachy, and I'd like to go to bed.'

'Of course.' Margaret was all sympathy. 'You've had a long journey, and travelling's always tiring.'

Ross had risen at the same time as Cathy and, standing by her side, his height dwarfing her, he suggested blandly, 'Perhaps you didn't get enough sleep last night?'

Ignoring the seemingly innocent remark, she murmured a general goodnight and on legs that felt as limp as a rag doll's headed blindly for the door.

But, without appearing to hurry, Ross reached it first and opened it for her.

On the surface it was merely a polite gesture, but he held the door in such a way that she couldn't actually go through it until he allowed her to.

A glint in his eye telling her he wasn't about to let her escape so easily, he remarked, 'I'd like you to be in my study tomorrow morning by eight o'clock—'

'*Your* study?' she broke in, startled, unable to hide her shock.

'That's right.'

'Oh, but I—I thought...' Taking a deep breath, she started again. 'I didn't realize...'

His eyes as cold and grey as the Atlantic in winter, he told her, 'It's the estate's office work and accounts that you'll be doing.'

'Oh…' she said hollowly. 'I presumed I would be working over at the lodge.'

He shook his head. 'Marley and Janet between them do everything that's necessary at Beinn Mor—'

Her face sympathetic, Janet broke in quickly, 'Don't worry, I'll be there to help until you get the hang of it.'

Frowning, Ross said brusquely, 'I understood from Marley that she would try to engage someone who was able to cope with the work.'

'I can cope,' Cathy said a shade defiantly.

It wasn't the thought of doing the accounts that was worrying her—she had worked for a firm of accountants since leaving school—but if she had to work at Dunbar it might mean running into *him*, and that was the last thing she wanted.

Margaret, who had noted her brother's unusual curtness and Cathy's look of dismay, jumped into the breach. 'I'm sure you can cope, but you may need just a bit of help to start with. You see, old Hector McDonald, who's been doing the paperwork for the best part of fifty years, has just retired. He was almost eighty-five and hadn't been up to the job for quite a while.

'Janet did what she could to keep things straight, but Hector refused to let her use "newfangled" methods—by which he meant a computer. Because he's been at Dunbar all his life, Ross was loath to hurt his feelings by insisting. Which means there's an awful lot to catch up on.'

'Hence the need to make an early start…' Ross took control once more.

Then, making Cathy look at him by sheer force of will, he went on, 'So I suggest you take a couple of painkillers and try to get a good night's sleep.'

'I always knew you were a slave-driver,' Kevin told his

brother-in-law banteringly, 'but I didn't have you down as a spoilsport.' With a broad grin, he added, 'Being a bachelor, *you* might have an empty bed, but don't forget Cathy and Carl are newlyweds who've been separated for a while... They'll no doubt have something better to do than sleep...'

Seeing the colour pour into Cathy's face, Margaret protested, 'Honestly, you men! Now you've made the poor girl blush.'

Ross's smile was derisive. 'As most couples live together before they get married, I find it surprising that any of today's worldly young women are still able to blush.'

Frowning at her brother, Margaret said, 'I don't know what's got into you tonight. It isn't like you to be so insensitive.'

Meeting Cathy's eyes, Ross murmured blandly, 'Of course if I've upset Mrs Richardson in any way...?'

Lifting her chin, Cathy answered as evenly as possible. 'I'm not at all upset... Now, if you'll excuse me...'

Remembering that he was supposed to be an eager young husband, Carl rose to his feet somewhat belatedly and asked Cathy, 'Do you want me to come with you, darling?'

'No... No, you stay and enjoy the company.'

'Do you have your keys?'

Cathy shook her head.

'In that case you'd better take mine.' He tossed them to her. 'You can leave the door on the latch for me... I'm out all day tomorrow with an inexperienced group of skiers, which means a fairly early start, so I won't be too late.'

'Well, goodnight, everyone,' Cathy murmured. Carefully avoiding looking at Ross, she pushed past the barrier of his arm and fled back to the flat.

Once in her room she sank down on the bed and let the tide of misery wash over her.

She had thanked fate for bringing Ross into her life, but all the time cruel fate—knowing what was in store—had been laughing up its sleeve.

As well it might.

Everything lay in ruins around her. Her newly found happiness, her hopes and dreams for the future, even the memories would be unbearable.

And what about Carl? *His* newly found happiness? *His* hopes and dreams for the future?

Once Ross told his sister about last night…

But even as the thought went through her mind she knew with certainty that he wouldn't. He wasn't that kind of man.

Briefly, she toyed with the idea of trying to explain, of telling him the truth.

But of course she couldn't.

There was no way she could expect him to keep quiet when his own family were being deceived.

For the time being at least she would have to let him go on thinking that she had the morals of an alley cat—that, even newly married, she would jump into bed with any available man.

Remembering the icy contempt and distaste that she had seen in his eyes, she shivered.

Suppose she told Carl what had happened last night? How much it meant to her? He wouldn't want her to go on with the deception.

But, recalling how glad and happy Carl had looked, she knew there was no way she could take her happiness at the expense of his.

And in any case, even if she could tell Ross the truth—that she was a cheat and a liar rather than an adulteress—it was too late.

Already the magic, the instant rapport that had sprung into

life between them, had died. A brief and beautiful spark that could never be rekindled.

The tears started to run down her cheeks, but almost savagely she dashed them away. No one, especially Carl, must see that she had been crying.

Her own chance of happiness was irretrievably lost, but if she could carry on as if nothing had happened until Carl was able to tell everyone the truth, *his* might be saved.

Then she could go quietly back to London and set about making a new life for herself. She'd done it once, after her parents had died, and she could and would do it again.

But she would never be able to recapture the singing happiness that meeting Ross had brought her.

Her movements slow and heavy, like those of a very old woman, she undressed, cleaned her teeth, brushed her hair and climbed wearily into bed.

More than two hours later, tormented by reoccurring thoughts of what might have been, she was still wide awake when she heard Carl come in.

He called her name softly, but, feeling unable to face him, she lay quietly without answering.

It was the early hours of the morning when, physically and mentally exhausted, her mind still full of images of Ross, she finally fell into a restless sleep.

CHAPTER FOUR

WHEN Cathy awoke, those images of Ross still filled her head, and just for a fleeting moment or two she felt blissfully happy and confident.

Then memory rushed in, reminding her of the cruel trick that fate had played on her. Her spirits fell to zero, and misery sidled up and took her hand.

Used to waking early, she hadn't set the alarm on her small bedside clock, and she was horrified to find it was almost a quarter to nine.

The flat was silent, and she guessed that Carl must have breakfasted and gone to work some time ago.

Stumbling out of bed, she hurried into the bathroom to clean her teeth and shower. Then, still feeling headachy and unrefreshed, she pulled on clean undies, a donkey-brown skirt and jumper and a russet-coloured suede jerkin.

Having brushed and pinned up her hair in record time, she dropped the flat keys into her jerkin pocket and hurried along to the study, ready to apologize to Janet for her tardiness.

As she approached the door there was a sudden flurry of movement, a soft pattering of velvet paws, and a large, imposing cat appeared by her side.

He was the colour of golden marmalade and beautifully

marked, with a white chest and legs, and an orange and white ringed tail.

The lower half of his face was a snowy white which ended in an inverted V above his nose, while the upper part of his head and his ears were a deep golden-orange, making him look as if he was wearing a batman-style helmet.

Cathy, who liked cats, exclaimed, 'Well, hello, where did you spring from?'

Looking up at her with big, clear eyes the pale greeny-gold of quartz, he opened his mouth in a silent miaow.

Stooping to stroke him, she observed, 'My, but you're a handsome boy.'

Apparently pleased by the compliment, he began to wind sinuously around her slender ankles. His fur was thick and soft, and he held his luxuriant tail aloft like a royal standard.

Her hand on the doorknob, she said, 'I don't know whether you're allowed in here, so you'd better make yourself scarce.'

Looking affronted, he fell back a step or two, but as she opened the door he darted in ahead of her and settled himself in front of the fire, where he sat with his back to her, aloof and reproachful.

Closing the door, she began, 'I'm sorry, I don't know whether...'

The apology died on her lips as she found herself looking into Ross's cold grey eyes rather than Janet's warm brown ones.

Sitting at the computer, his face hard, his jaw set, he glanced pointedly at his watch.

'I—I'm sorry,' she stammered. 'I overslept.'

'So I see. I'd rather hoped that this time Marley had found a couple who were decent and reliable. But it seems I was wrong on both counts.'

Stiffly, she said, 'I can assure you it won't happen again. In future I'll take good care to set the alarm.'

'There may not *be* a future if your husband has messed up the day's arrangements by being late.'

'I'm sure Carl wouldn't have been late.'

'What time did he leave?'

'I—I don't really know.'

'You didn't hear him go?'

She shook her head. 'I must have been asleep.'

'And he didn't wake you?'

'He probably didn't think it was necessary. He's used to me being up fairly early.'

'What time *did* you get up?'

'It was a quarter to nine,' she admitted reluctantly. 'But I hadn't had much sleep and…'

Suddenly recalling Kevin's joking remark about newlyweds having something better to do than sleep, she flushed scarlet.

Watching the colour flood into her face, Ross drawled, 'Of course, when you've had to make do with a substitute…'

Hearing the underlying bitterness, she whispered, 'I'm sorry. Truly I am. I only wish I could change what happened—'

'I'm sure you do,' he said bitingly. 'After you'd gone last night Marley said how much she liked you and described you as quiet and sweet and rather shy. The others agreed. And your husband, who obviously thinks the world of you, added that you were loyal and very special and he was a lucky man to have you in his life. I wonder how he and the others would react if they knew the rather sordid truth?'

Through dry lips, she asked, 'Were you thinking of telling them?'

'That all depends.'

'On what?'

'If you do exactly as I tell you, and don't get up to any tricks with Beinn Mor's male guests, for your husband's sake I'm prepared to keep quiet and give you a chance.'

'You mean I'm on probation?'

'You catch on quickly,' he told her sardonically. 'But then just because you're a wanton, it doesn't mean that you're not intelligent enough.'

Watching every trace of colour drain from her face, he said, 'I take it the word *wanton* offends you? But I'm afraid that when a newly married woman acts in the way you did, I can't think of a kinder one…'

'I…I don't…' There was a roaring in her ears, and the room began to swirl around her.

Ross moved quickly and caught her as she swayed. A supporting arm around her, he steered her to one of the armchairs in front of the fire and, having lowered her gently into it, pressed her head down to her knees.

After a few seconds the faintness began to pass, and, lifting her head, she managed shakily, 'Thank you, I'm fine now.'

He looked down at her.

She was white to the lips, and her eyes appeared to be too big for her pale face.

'You don't look fine,' he said curtly. 'You look like a ghost. Did you have any breakfast?'

'No.'

'When was the last time you sat down to a meal?'

'Last night.'

'Last night you scarcely ate a thing. What about lunchtime? Did you stop on the way here?'

She shook her head.

'So you've had nothing to eat since breakfast yesterday—if then…?'

She didn't answer, but, reading her expression correctly, he said impatiently, 'Have you no sense? Your blood sugar must be so low it's a wonder you haven't passed out before now.'

Striding over to the mantelpiece, he pressed a bell. A short time later there was a tap at the door and the young maid who had served dinner the previous evening appeared.

'Ah, Flora,' he addressed the girl pleasantly, 'will you please ask Cook to send a tray of toast and honey and a pot of coffee?'

'Yes, sir.' With a little bob, she turned and hurried away.

Dropping into the chair opposite Cathy's, Ross looked at her, his expression unreadable.

Then, taking her by surprise, his tone despairing rather than angry, he demanded, 'Newly married to a decent man like Carl—what made you do it?'

She half shook her head. 'I'm sorry... I only wish I could explain.'

'There's no need to, really. It's self-explanatory. Too many hormones and too little self-control.'

His mouth twisting in the semblance of a smile, he added, 'When I met you, I thought you were different, special... And because of the way you responded to me, like a fool I fondly imagined that you felt the same way about me.'

Then savagely he said, 'Have you the faintest idea what it feels like to think you've found near perfection and then discover you've been made a fool of, that the woman you thought so highly of is just a cheating little bitch...?'

Caught on the raw, she flashed, 'And I suppose you've never cheated?'

'No, I haven't,' he answered uncompromisingly. 'While I was engaged I never looked at anyone else, and if I ever get married the same will apply. I have to admit that when there's no special woman around I don't live like a monk. But I've always drawn the line at getting involved with anyone who was married. Now I find myself in the invidious position of having slept with an employee's wife.'

For perhaps the first time she realized just how deep his anger and disillusionment went.

As she recalled the gentle passion he had shown her that night, the warmth and melting sweetness of his lovemaking, a giant hand seemed to tighten round her heart.

Desperate to wipe that terrible bleakness from his face, she wished yet again that she could tell him the truth.

But it was no use, she thought despairingly. It wouldn't solve anything. What he had felt for her had gone for ever. He would never again feel the same.

Fighting back tears, she repeated unhappily, 'I'm sorry… I'd better leave…'

'What good would that do?' he asked curtly. 'You couldn't leave without giving a reason. And if you told your husband the truth, apart from destroying whatever trust he has in you, it would mean depriving him of a job that he obviously wants, and leaving Marley and Kevin in the lurch… No, I think we'll both have to live with what happened and—'

He stopped speaking as a tap at the door heralded the arrival of the maid with a tray. When she had placed it on the coffee table, she asked, 'Will that be all, sir?'

'Yes, thank you, Flora.'

When the door had closed behind the girl, Ross filled two cups with the fragrant coffee before turning his attention to the toast.

Having spread a slice liberally with butter and honey, he set the plate in front of Cathy. 'There… Let me see you eat that.'

About to say that she disliked honey, Cathy thought better of it and, under his uncompromising gaze, managed to force the toast down between sips of coffee.

As he reached to spread another slice, she said hastily, 'I really can't eat any more... But I would like another cup of coffee, please.'

He had just finished pouring it when the phone on his desk rang.

'Excuse me,' he said with formal politeness, and went to pick up the receiver.

While he and the caller held a low-toned conversation, Cathy drank the coffee and tried, without much success, to get a grip on her emotions.

She had just reached to put the cup and saucer on the table, when the cat, who had been washing himself with fastidious care, rose to his feet, stretched stiff-legged and then, to show he'd forgiven her, leapt gracefully into her lap.

Feeling wretched and still perilously close to tears, Cathy found it a comfort to have something warm and alive to stroke.

He had just rolled onto his back, presenting a spotless white tummy to be tickled, when Ross came back to stand in front of the fire.

Frowning a little, he asked, 'How long have you and Onions been acquainted?'

Her voice a little husky, Cathy said, 'We met just now in the hall.'

'I must say I was somewhat startled when he came in with you.'

'I'm sorry... I wasn't sure if he was allowed in your study, but—'

'No, no, that isn't what I meant.' With a crooked grin, he added, 'It's just that he's very much a lone-wolf type of cat, if you see what I mean...'

Just for an instant she glimpsed the Ross she had first met, and her heart turned over.

'He usually won't have any truck with strangers. Or anyone

else for that matter. He tolerates the cook because she feeds him, and the rest of the household because he must, but so far I'm the only one he's allowed to get close to him. My ex-fiancée tried to make friends and got bitten for her pains. But he seems to have taken a fancy to you.'

His tone, though far from friendly, was neutral enough to encourage her to ask, 'You said his name was Onions?'

'Yes.'

The monosyllable was somewhat daunting, but still she pressed on, 'It's an unusual name for a cat.'

'There's a reason for it…'

She had just decided he wasn't going to tell her what that reason was, when he went on, 'A couple of years ago I was on my way here from London, and I stopped at a service station for a coffee. When I returned to the car, I heard what I first thought was a young baby mewling. Then I realized the sound was coming from an old cardboard box that had been tossed down beside a litter bin. I looked inside and there was this tiny bedraggled kitten. From the dried tops and skins he was lying on, it was apparent that the box had been used for storing onions.

'He was so weak from starvation I didn't think he'd survive. But once I'd managed to get some warm milk inside him—a woman in the service station café kindly sacrificed one of her baby's spare feeding bottles—he rallied and never looked back.

'Marley was trying to think of a suitable name for him when she noticed that on one of his white hind legs he had two small oval patches of pale orange that looked remarkably like dried shallots. That, coupled with the debris in the box, made us start to call him Onions *pro tem*. But somehow the name stuck.'

A smile lit up Cathy's face as, momentarily forgetting her woes, she remarked, 'Though the name Onions seems a bit undignified for a cat with so much character, oddly enough, it suits him.'

Seeing that smile, Ross tightened his mouth into a hard line, and, rising abruptly to his feet, he said, 'If you're feeling better it's high time we both got some work done.'

'Yes, of course. Come on, Onions…'

'First, I've got some business to attend to that has nothing to do with the estate,' Ross told her. 'But presumably, as you said you could cope, you have some bookkeeping experience?'

'Yes.'

'And you can use a computer?'

'Of course.'

'Then, as I've made a start, you should be able to get on for an hour or so without me.'

'I'm quite capable of working alone on a permanent basis,' she informed him stiffly.

Not giving an inch, he retorted, 'I hope you'll allow me to be the judge of that.'

Without another word, he added fresh pine logs to the fire and, escorted by Onions, departed, closing the door behind him.

Cathy went over to the desk and, struggling to push aside all thoughts but those of work, settled herself to carry on where Ross had left off.

Though the handwritten accounts were slightly spidery, they proved to be clear and painstakingly correct, so it was child's play to transfer them to the computer.

Determined to show Ross that as far as the job was concerned he couldn't fault her, she worked steadily until there was a tap at the door.

In answer to her, 'Come in,' Flora appeared, carrying a tray of coffee and sandwiches and a bowl of mixed fruit.

'Mr Dalgowan asked me to bring you this…'

Smiling at the girl, she said, 'Thank you, Flora. If you'd like to put it on the coffee table?'

When she'd done as she was bidden, with a little bob the maid scurried away.

Having moved to sit by the fire, Cathy poured a cup of coffee and helped herself to a ham and salad sandwich. It was delicious and, her usual healthy appetite reasserting itself, she ate the rest of the sandwiches before peeling an orange.

As soon as she had finished, she slipped along to the flat to wash her hands.

When she went back to the study, she found the tray had gone and the fire had been made up.

Returning to the computer, she stayed there until it began to get dark and she was forced to pause and switch on the light.

That done, she resumed work, her concentration such that she lost all track of time.

When the phone began to ring, she jumped.

Reaching to pick up the receiver, she said a cautious, 'Hello?'

'Where are you?' Carl's voice asked.

'In Mr Dalgowan's study.'

'You're not still working? Have you any idea what time it is?'

A quick glance at her watch showed it was almost a quarter to seven. The fire had died down, and she was stiff from sitting in one position.

'I didn't realize it was so late,' she admitted.

'With not seeing you this morning,' Carl went on, 'I forgot to mention that on Saturday nights there's always an après-ski party at Beinn Mor. So, when you've had time to change into your party frock, I'll pop up for you.'

Though she felt tired and had a dull headache, knowing that it would look odd if she didn't join Carl, she agreed, 'Right, I'll be ready.'

She saved the work she had done, turned off the computer and hurried back to the flat.

When she tried to fit the key into the lock, she found that the door wasn't closed properly and it moved under the slight pressure.

Carl must already be there. He'd obviously come straight over and left the door open for her. 'I'm back,' she called. 'I'll be as quick as I can.'

There was no answer, and a glance in the various rooms soon confirmed that, apart from herself, the flat was empty.

Of course! Carl had mentioned that sometimes the door failed to latch, and that must have happened when she'd left at lunchtime.

But, thinking back, she was certain she *had* closed it properly. She could remember hearing the latch click into place.

Perhaps Carl had popped back for something during the afternoon?

No, surely he'd been out all day?

Then maybe the maid had come in, after all?

But everything was just as she had left it. Carl's breakfast dishes were still unwashed, the used towels were still in a damp pile in the bathroom and neither of the beds had been made.

Oh, well, it was no use worrying about it. If someone *had* been in, no harm had been done...

And she must get a move on.

Dropping the keys into her shoulder bag, she made herself an instant coffee and swallowed a couple of aspirins, before showering quickly.

That done, she donned a silky cocktail dress in soft shades of grey and lavender with a slightly flared skirt and a scooped neckline.

The simple cut showed off her slender waist, the curve of

her breasts, and somewhat more of her cleavage than she was totally comfortable with. But it was the only party dress she had, so it would have to do.

Knowing the journey would be door to door, she decided on court shoes rather than boots, which might prove too warm for a party.

Lightly made up to hide her paleness, she took her hair into a smooth, gleaming coil and fastened small gold hoops to her lobes.

She had just slipped into a cream hooded jacket with a soft suede finish—a fashion statement rather than a serious winter outfit—and picked up her bag, when Carl appeared in the doorway.

'You look great,' he commented with approval. 'Though with shoes like that I may have to carry you to the car.'

'Had I better…?' Suddenly noticing *his* lightweight footwear, she stopped and demanded, 'What about you?'

'If I need them I have boots and all the necessary winter equipment over at the lodge… And I was only joking about the shoes… Your chariot awaits you right outside the door, so you'll be fine as you are.'

Snowflakes were drifting and eddying, soft as a lover's caress, as they got into the car and drove the short distance to Beinn Mor.

When they drew up at the lodge the scene was truly festive, with the glittering Christmas tree, coloured lanterns bobbing slightly in the freshening breeze and strings of fairy lights blinking and twinkling through the falling snow.

The muted sound of music and laughter and revelry issuing forth into the snowy night made it abundantly clear that the après-ski party was already well under way.

'Isn't it all lovely and festive?' Cathy remarked as they drew up by the porch.

'You wait until Christmas Eve. I've been told that every year there's a Christmas Eve ball held in the main hall at Dunbar. Even the old laird, who apparently was a dour man, kept it up. A band comes all the way from Keiltullich, a firm of caterers decorate and provide a buffet supper, and it's open house. Everyone from Beinn Mor, and all the locals for miles around, put on their glad rags and come.'

'It sounds fun.'

'I've no doubt it will be,' he assured her as he helped her out.

As soon as they got inside, a red-coated Santa with the customary hat and white whiskers approached them. Well into the spirit of the part, and booming 'Ho! Ho! Ho!', he was carrying a sack containing lucky-dip gifts.

When they had each drawn out a small, gaily wrapped parcel, they left them, along with their outdoor things and Cathy's bag, in the nearby cloakroom.

When they returned to the party, Margaret and Janet spotted them and gave a friendly wave.

The two woman were talking, and as Carl headed in their direction Cathy heard Margaret say, 'I'd half expected Lena to turn up. The last time I saw her she said she'd be visiting her father before Christmas… And you know what that means…'

Janet grimaced. 'I can't help but wonder if she's still a bit in love with Ross. She can't seem to let go, more's the pity…'

Turning to smile at them both, Margaret said, 'Hi! It looks like being a good evening. People are mixing well, and Kevin is into his stride as DJ…'

Through the open doors that led into the next room, Cathy could see that the floor had been cleared for dancing, and at the far end a dinner-jacketed Kevin was selecting disks to go into the player.

After chatting for a while, Janet and Margaret moved away

to circulate, and, trying to put all thoughts of Ross and his ex-fiancée out of her mind, Cathy glanced around.

The majority of the women wore cocktail dresses, while the men tended to go for smart après-ski wear.

One or two couples were already dancing, while others sat and watched as they sipped their drinks.

In the foyer-cum-lounge the bar was doing a brisk business, and a substantial buffet had been set out on a series of trestle tables.

People were standing around in small groups, drinks in their hands, laughing and cheerful as they talked animatedly about the day's skiing.

Listening to them as they compared the snow and weather conditions to previous holidays, it soon became obvious to Cathy that they belonged to a kind of skiing fraternity that met up each year.

From the look on Carl's face, she could see that the talk and the camaraderie were meat and drink to him, and that he wanted nothing more than to be a part of this world.

As though becoming conscious of her gaze, he turned to her and suggested, 'What about a dance?'

Well aware that he'd never cared much for dancing, she asked, 'Wouldn't you rather be with your skiing companions talking about the day's excitements?'

He grinned wryly. 'How well you know me. But it might look strange if we don't have at least one dance together.'

The atmosphere of fun and gaiety was infectious and lifted her enough to make her say lightly, 'In that case, let's go.'

The music was a mixture of older and newer tunes, and they danced to a couple of lively numbers. As the last one ended, Carl suggested, 'Would you like a drink? If I can get anywhere near the bar, that is.'

'If you can, I'll have a glass of dry white wine. But if there's too much of a scrum, don't bother.'

Then as he turned to go she added quickly, 'By the way, there's no need to hurry back. Circulate a bit—I'll be fine.'

'Well, if you're sure?'

'I'm sure.'

He gave her a grateful look and disappeared into the throng.

She listened to the music for a little while, then rather than stand around like the proverbial wallflower she decided to make her way into the other room and sit—unobtrusively, she hoped—in front of the fire.

She had taken only a couple of steps when a tall, sturdily built man with brown receding hair and a pleasant, open face, appeared by her side.

He smiled at her somewhat shyly and said, 'Good evening, Mrs Richardson.'

Recognizing him as Robert Munro, Dunbar's estate manager, she smiled back and returned his greeting, adding, 'But won't you call me Cathy?'

'I'd like to, if you'll call me Robert.'

'Agreed.'

His hazel eyes still a shade diffident, he went on in his soft Scottish brogue, 'I just had a word with your husband, and he mentioned that he'd temporarily deserted you. As you don't really know anyone yet, I thought it might be a bit lonely for you...' Then in a rush he said, 'I wondered if you'd like to dance?'

Thinking what a genuinely nice man he was, she agreed, 'Yes, I'd love to.'

'Would you mind very much if we wait a few seconds to see what the next song is going to be?'

'Of course not.'

When an old favourite began, looking distinctly embarrassed, he confessed, 'I'm afraid I'm not what you'd call a great dancer.'

'Don't worry about that,' Cathy said quickly. 'I'm not very good at it either, but let's give it a go.'

Taking his hand, she urged him onto the floor. 'There's no need to do anything fancy. All we have to do is move to the beat.'

He pulled a comical face. 'Somehow it seems harder than that.'

Laughing, she said, 'It isn't, I promise.'

At that instant she caught sight of Ross, looking devastatingly handsome in a well-cut dinner jacket. His eyes were fixed on them, and, feeling guilty for no reason at all, she wondered how long he had been standing there watching them both.

Her companion gave no sign that he had noticed that cold gaze, and, taking great care not to look in Ross's direction, Cathy made an effort to dismiss him from her mind.

After a few seconds, Robert got the hang of the beat and gave quite a creditable performance.

'There you are!' Cathy exclaimed triumphantly. 'What did I tell you?'

Looking greatly relieved, he admitted, 'In a way it's easier than ballroom dancing, but I've never had the nerve to try before.'

They stayed on the floor for another number and then a quickstep was announced.

With a sheepish grin, Robert said, 'I'd love to keep on, but I have to warn you I'm not very good at ballroom dancing either. Though I know what I *should* do, I seem to have two left feet.'

Cathy, who had relaxed with this kind, unassuming man, said, 'Well, I'm game if you are, and we'll see who's the first to tread on their partner's toes.'

When they had circled the floor a couple of times without anything amiss happening, Robert beamed at her and said, 'Thanks very much for all your encouragement. I can't remember when I've enjoyed myself so much.' Then he added hastily, 'But I don't want to monopolize you, so promise you'll tell me when you've had enough…'

'I promise,' she said gravely.

'And of course there's your husband to consider. I'd hate him to be angry with you.'

'I can assure you he won't be that,' she said lightly. 'In fact I'm quite certain he'll be happy that you're taking care of me.'

Partly because it kept her from having to make conversation—which could be uncomfortable and might involve lying—and partly because as a companion Robert was easy and unthreatening, she, too, was enjoying herself, and she would willingly have danced with him all evening.

'The next number,' Kevin announced through the microphone, 'will be a gentlemen's "excuse me".'

It was a modern waltz, and they had taken just a few steps, when a man tapped Robert on the shoulder.

Relinquishing his partner with a formal little bow, Robert made his way off the floor, and Cathy found herself face to face with a man she had never set eyes on before.

CHAPTER FIVE

HER first feeling was one of relief. Just for an instant she had feared the newcomer was Ross.

But this man was nothing like Ross.

Somewhere in his mid-thirties, she guessed, he was tall and beefy, good-looking in a florid, flashy kind of way, with dark wavy hair and bold blue eyes.

He held her much too close and smelt of whisky and expensive aftershave.

'At last,' he said, with a London accent and an unappealing brashness. 'I've been waiting for a chance to get to know you.'

Cathy said nothing, and after a moment he went on, his voice over-loud, 'I haven't seen you around, and with a face and figure like yours I would certainly have remembered if I had.'

When she remained silent and aloof, he persisted, 'My name's Nigel Cunningham. What's yours?'

'Cathy,' she answered reluctantly.

'Which party are you with, Cathy?'

'I'm not with any party,' she said with cool politeness. 'I work here.'

'Do you, indeed? What's your job? I hope it's being nice to the male guests.'

'I'm afraid not.'

'So what *do* they pay you for?'

Already disliking him intensely, and willing the dance to end so she could escape, she said as civilly as possible, 'I work in the office.'

'Doing what? Keeping the boss-man happy?'

'Sitting in front of a computer.'

'A looker like you! What a waste of talent.'

He was slurring his words slightly, and she realized with a sinking heart that he'd already had far too much to drink.

A covered, glassed-in veranda ran along the rear of the lodge, and because the room was fairly full and growing over-warm, one of the French windows that led onto it had been propped open.

Starting to feel hot and agitated, Cathy was welcoming the flow of cooler air when her dancing partner exclaimed, 'Hell's bells! Are they trying to freeze us out?' Then with a confident leer he said, 'Never mind, baby, stick with me and I'll keep you warm.'

Holding her even closer, he let his hand slip down from her waist to cup one buttock.

Bearing in mind that he was almost certainly a guest, she bit back the urge to pull away and smack his face and said through gritted teeth, 'Will you please keep your hand where it belongs?'

Giving her a little squeeze, he asked thickly, 'Why so stand-offish?'

'Mr Cunningham, will you please do as I ask?'

'Come on, it's the festive season.'

Unwilling to cause a scene, she stopped dancing and said in a low, angry voice, 'For the last time, *will* you let go of me?'

'You don't really mean that,' he wheedled.

'I certainly do mean it.'

'Relax, baby—'

Seeing that words were useless, she pulled herself free

and, making her way through the couples still dancing, headed for the door.

A crowd of revellers with drinks in their hands were blocking the doorway, laughing uproariously at some story one of the group was telling.

Rather than trying to push her way through, she sheered off and circled the edge of the room until she reached the open French window.

Slipping through it, she moved a little way along the lantern-strung veranda. Though she could still hear the music, she was beyond the range of the main lights and out of sight of anyone in the room.

Tables and chairs had been placed at intervals, and at either end of the veranda a glowing space heater took off the worst of the chill for any hardy souls who wanted to spend a few minutes admiring the view.

But so far there had been no takers, and Cathy had the veranda to herself.

Breathing a sigh of relief, she drank in the cooler air as she stood and stared through the glass at the snow-covered foothills and the magnificent backdrop of higher mountains.

Snow was still falling steadily, piling up against the panes, shrouding the trees and bushes and weighing down the green boughs of the pines—boughs that were starting to heave and thrash about in the rising wind.

Ever since she was a child Cathy had loved all aspects of the weather, and it was such a beautiful, exciting scene that for a short time she forgot the distasteful little incident that had driven her out there.

Then an arm snaked around her waist, and that hated voice said in her ear, 'Playing hard to get, huh? Come on, baby, that doesn't cut any ice with me. Loosen up...'

'Let me go!'

Pulling away, she tried to push past him, but he grabbed hold of her and, his voice thickening, muttered, 'You're the most gorgeous woman I've ever seen and I need you to be nice to me...'

Then he was kissing her, his lips hot and wet and rubbery, his breath reeking of whisky, his hands all over her.

'Damn you, let her go.' Though quietly spoken, the words cut like a lash.

A second later Cathy was abruptly released as her unwanted admirer was plucked away.

Shuddering, wiping the back of her hand across her mouth, she found herself looking into Ross Dalgowan's angry face.

Bearing in mind the semi-drunken state he was in, Nigel Cunningham's recovery was fast. Bristling, he demanded belligerently, 'Who the hell do you think you're talking to?'

'You.' Both Ross's tone and his manner were uncompromising. 'Now, get out of here, before I'm tempted to break your neck.'

Taking an aggressive step forward, Cunningham jeered, 'Let's just see you try!' No doubt made reckless by the drink, he aimed a punch at the other man's jaw.

He was as tall as Ross and several stone heavier, and if the punch had connected it might have done some considerable damage.

But Ross sidestepped neatly and it swung harmlessly past his ear.

Carried forward by the impetus, Cunningham went sprawling heavily, ignominiously, on the wooden floor of the veranda.

Struggling to his feet, he lunged at his adversary.

The next minute he found himself propelled backwards by a single hand and pushed none too gently against the wall.

Sobered somewhat by the ease with which he had been bested, but not yet ready to admit defeat, he snarled, 'I don't know what all the fuss is about! What harm is there in a little kiss? Damn it, there's bunches of mistletoe hanging all over the place.'

His voice glacial, Ross pointed out, 'That wasn't just a Christmas kiss under the mistletoe, as well you know.'

'Well, what if it wasn't? She's enough to tempt any man to try his luck.'

'So you were "trying your luck"?'

'What if I was? If the lady was willing to have some fun, what business is it of yours?' Then, light dawning, he said, 'Oh, I see, you fancied your own chances and you're jealous!'

Ignoring the accusation of jealousy, Ross said coldly, 'Perhaps "the lady" failed to tell you that she's employed here?'

Desperate to escape the unpleasant little scene, Cathy was edging towards the French windows when Ross ordered grimly, 'Stay where you are. I want a word with you.'

As he had moved to block her way, she had little choice but to obey.

'Well, what if she is employed here?' Cunningham demanded. 'She told me she works in the office, so she wasn't on duty.'

'Whether she was "on duty" or not isn't relevant. It's Beinn Mor's policy not to allow members of the staff to fool around with the guests *at any time*. So leave her alone.'

'Policy be damned!' he blustered. 'There was no problem last year, and I've paid good money to come here again and have some fun. So don't imagine you can come along dishing out orders.' Then with rising indignation he demanded, 'Who the hell do you think you are, anyway?'

'My name's Dalgowan, and I happen to be the owner of the Dunbar Estate, and that includes the Ski Lodge. So you'd better listen to me when I tell you to keep well away from Mrs Richardson, otherwise—'

'*Mrs* Richardson?'

'Oh, yes. But no doubt that wouldn't worry a man of your type.'

'She never said a word about being married,' Cunningham protested.

Ross reached for her left hand. 'Heavens above, man, can't you see—' He broke off abruptly, and a white line appeared round his mouth.

Following his gaze, Cathy realized with a shock of horror that her left hand was bare. Her mother's ring had gone.

Dropping her hand, Ross turned back to Cunningham and said crisply, 'As Mrs Richardson forgot to wear her wedding ring, I accept that what happened just now may not have been entirely your fault. However, let me give you some advice: if you want to enjoy the rest of your stay, you'd better tread your shoes straight, otherwise...'

He left the threat unfinished, but Cunningham, who had clearly had enough, turned and shambled away.

As he reached the French windows, he rallied enough to say with what dignity he could muster, 'I suppose you realize that after being spoken to in that manner, I'll never come here again.'

'Which is just as well,' Ross informed him flatly. 'You wouldn't be welcome.'

When the other man had disappeared from sight, Ross, his face set, turned to Cathy and, his voice quietly furious, said, 'I warned you not to get up to any tricks with the guests, and then I find you kissing one of them.'

Shivering now, partly with cold and partly with stress, she objected, 'I wasn't kissing him. *He* was kissing *me*.'

'A fine distinction.'

'It's the truth.'

Lifting a level brow, he said sardonically, 'So you're asking me to believe that you were more sinned against than sinning?'

'I'm asking you to believe that I couldn't help what happened.'

'Don't come the innocent with me. I saw you dancing together before you came out here with him.'

'If you were watching you must know that I didn't come out here with him. I came out alone and he followed me.'

'Of course. In the circumstances you must have deemed it a necessary strategy.'

'It was nothing of the kind,' she denied hotly. 'I thought he was an obnoxious man. I was doing my best to get away from him.'

'I might *possibly* have believed that if I hadn't seen you together on the dance floor. When he started getting…shall we say over-familiar?…you made no attempt to stop him.'

'That's where you're wrong! I tried to stop him, but he wouldn't listen to me.'

'You didn't look as if you were trying very hard.'

'What did you expect me to do? Slap his face in the middle of the dance floor? As far as I was concerned he was a paying guest here and I didn't want to cause a scene…'

'If I believed that, I would applaud such noble self-sacrifice. But as you appeared to be enjoying his attentions—'

'You're quite mistaken!' she said hotly. 'How *could* you think I was enjoying being made the target of some drunken Casanova who…' Her voice wobbled dangerously, and she stopped speaking.

'I must congratulate you on your acting ability. If I didn't already know what kind of woman you are, I might be convinced by your vehemence.'

'You *don't* know what kind of woman I am.'

'Oh, I think I do,' he said, contempt in his voice. 'There's only one kind of woman who would hide the fact that she's newly married and jump into bed with a man she'd only just met. A man,' he added caustically, 'who meant absolutely nothing to her except possibly a cheap sexual thrill…'

Cathy had opened her mouth to refute the latter statement but, realizing she couldn't, she bit her lip and stayed silent.

Noting that silence, Ross went on, 'The kind of woman who, having been warned not to get up to any tricks, deliberately encourages an obvious lecher like Cunningham—'

'I did nothing of the kind,' she cried. Then, in despair she said, 'Oh, why am I bothering? I'll never be able to convince you.'

'You could always try.'

'I'm getting cold.'

'Then we'll go somewhere warmer.'

'I don't want to go anywhere with you.'

She turned to head for the French windows, but he caught her arm.

Anger blinding her to the danger signals in his face, the tightening of the skin over his cheekbones, the set of his jaw, she cried, '*Will* you let me be? I've had enough of being manhandled for one night.'

'If you think for one minute that—'

He broke off abruptly as a couple appeared in the doorway and glanced at them curiously.

Knowing he couldn't detain her now, Cathy made the most of her opportunity. Pulling free, she brushed past him and was through the open door in an instant, the skirt of her dress swirling round her slim legs.

She had started to make her way round the edge of the room when, from behind, strong hands closed lightly around her upper arms and she was steered onto the dance floor.

It was a quickstep, and, turning her in his arms, Ross began to move lightly, easily, amongst the circling couples, leaving her no alternative but to follow him.

When, after a moment or two, that number came to an end, she made a fruitless attempt to free herself.

'If you don't let me go,' she hissed, 'this time I'm quite willing to cause a scene...'

Unimpressed, he said, 'I very much doubt it. There would be far too much awkward explaining to do.'

As he finished speaking, Kevin announced, 'Ladies and gentlemen, as we've had a fairly lively mixture so far, the next few dances are specially for all the lovers present.'

The lights were dimmed, and a moment later the soft, romantic strains of an old ballad filled the air.

The words had a certain poignant relevance, and Cathy bit her lip as, one hand imprisoning hers, the other at her slender waist, Ross drew her closer and started to dance.

Once again with no option, she followed his lead.

Though she was tall for a woman, he was appreciably taller, and her head fitted snugly beneath his chin.

Her heart was beating so hard with a combination of anger and other emotions she preferred not to define that she felt almost giddy.

At first she held herself stiff as a poker, until he bent his blond head and said in her ear, 'Why don't you unbend a little and try to enjoy it?'

He was a good dancer, lithe and easy to follow, and gradually the anger drained away, leaving a kind of melancholy weariness, an acceptance of the tricks fate seemed to be playing on her.

Eventually, with his hand moving in a slow caress up and down her spine, and his cheek resting lightly against her hair, she relaxed and, yearning for the truce he seemed to be offering, momentarily let her forehead rest against his chest.

His breath stirring a loose tendril of hair at her temple, he asked softly, mockingly, 'Trying your wiles on me again?'

The injustice of it stung like a nettle, and, missing a step, she stumbled slightly.

Then, pulling away from him as much as he would allow, she lifted her head and, her voice low and bewildered, said, 'That wasn't fair.'

'It wasn't meant to be.'

His cruel words and the coldness in his face, when she had been hoping for a lessening of hostilities, came as a blow.

Tears sprang into her beautiful eyes, making them gleam like the opals he'd likened them to.

He drew her hard against him and turned her so that his wide shoulders hid her from the majority of the couples dancing.

'Don't cry,' he said, his voice harsh.

She shook her head, and a fine strand of silky hair clung momentarily to his jacket as she denied fiercely, 'I'm not crying.'

But a single tear spilled over and rolled slowly down her cheek, making her a liar.

He released her hand just briefly to brush the glittering drop away with his thumb, before demanding with a sigh, 'Don't you care about your marriage at all? When you have a husband like Carl, why do you find it necessary to encourage every man you meet?'

'I've told you repeatedly, but you won't believe me, that I thought Nigel Cunningham was obnoxious, and I certainly never gave him any encouragement.'

'Just as you never gave *me* any encouragement?'

His face sardonic, he watched the colour rise in her cheeks and the downward sweep of her long lashes.

'But as it happens I wasn't talking about Cunningham. I was talking about Robert Munro. It's no use telling me you didn't encourage *him*. I was standing watching you. When he obviously didn't want to go on the dance floor, I saw you take hold of his hand to persuade him. So don't try to deny it.'

It struck her that he was reacting just like a jealous lover, and she might almost have believed Nigel Cunningham's accusation had it been anyone other than herself who was involved.

But, as it was, she knew all he felt for *her* was anger and contempt.

Taking a deep breath, she tried to explain. 'Robert is a thoroughly nice man and I like him. But though he enjoys dancing he lacks confidence. When I took hold of his hand I was encouraging him to dance. Nothing more. Ask him if you don't believe me…'

'How can I believe a woman who deliberately takes off her wedding ring so she can—?'

'I *didn't* take it off,' Cathy broke in hoarsely. 'I was wearing it when Carl and I left the flat earlier tonight.' Then in a sudden panic of realization she said, 'I must have lost it somewhere.'

Clearly not believing her, Ross drawled, 'Try again, sweetheart.'

'But it's the truth,' she insisted urgently.

His voice dismissive, he observed, 'Well, it can't mean much to you.'

'That's where you're wrong! It means a great deal to me. Much more than I can say.'

'Don't bother to lie,' he said wearily. 'If it really meant that much, you'd give up your alley cat ways and—'

He broke off as the dance came to an end.

At the same instant a man appeared at Ross's elbow and said, 'Excuse me, Mr Dalgowan, but when you've got a minute to spare, the man who's running the orienteering classes would like your advice…'

As Ross's grip loosened, trembling in every limb, Cathy pulled free and, brushing past the newcomer with a murmured, 'Excuse me,' hurriedly made her way through the crowd.

On reaching the foyer she glanced around, but could see no sign of Carl or anyone else she knew amongst the laughing, chattering throng.

Things were hotting up, and, knowing it was useless to start looking for the ring, suddenly bone-weary and at the end of her emotional tether, she wanted nothing more than to find her coat and go.

But first, so Carl wouldn't worry about her, she had to find someone to leave a message with.

All at once she spotted Janet, standing near the bar, and with some difficulty made her way over.

Janet greeted her with a warm smile and, having introduced her to the couple she was with, went on in her soft Scottish accent, 'If you're looking for Carl, he's in the morning room having a pow-wow with the New Venture Group. They're trying to make arrangements to fit in an overnight winter survival course before Christmas. So if you don't go and root him out you may not see him for hours.'

'It's all right,' Cathy said quickly. 'I won't disturb him. But if he should come looking for me, I'd be grateful if you'd tell him that I've gone back to the flat.'

'Oh, do you have to go?' Janet exclaimed. 'We haven't even had supper yet. Our après-ski parties usually go on until after midnight. Why don't you join us?'

Appreciating the other woman's kindness, Cathy said, 'Thanks, but I'd rather go. I've had a couple of bad nights, and I'm feeling really tired, so I'd like to get to bed.'

'Well, if that's what you want.'

'Yes, it is.'

'But how will you get back?' Janet asked in sudden concern. 'It's nearly a mile to Dunbar itself if you go by the main drive. That's much too far for you to walk in these conditions.'

'It's all right. Carl told me he has all his winter gear here, and he knows the shortcut, so I'll take the car.'

'You have the keys?'

'They'll be in his coat pocket... Oh, when you *do* see him, will you please tell him that I've got my own keys to the flat, so there's really no need for him to hurry back.'

'I'll tell him... By the way, as it's been snowing all evening, you'll go steady, won't you?'

'Of course,' Cathy assured her. 'Though it doesn't seem to have been coming down too fast.'

'It's surprising how quickly it accumulates, and because of the need to keep the trails to the cabins passable, the drive hasn't been properly cleared since yesterday.'

'It wasn't bad when we came,' Cathy told her. Then, seeing that the other woman was genuinely anxious, she added, 'But I promise I'll drive carefully.'

Janet smiled her relief. 'I hope you get a good night's sleep. Margaret was quite concerned to find that because the rest of us work Saturdays, Ross is expecting you to do the same.'

'Please tell her not to worry,' Cathy said as evenly as possible. 'It's only right that I should work the same hours as everyone else.'

As soon as they had said their goodnights, anxious to get away in case Ross caught up with her again, Cathy hurried to the cloakroom.

Looking back as she reached the door, she saw his blond head at the far side of the room and ducked in hastily, hoping he hadn't spotted her.

Having located both Carl's jacket and her own, she slipped hers on and put her bag over her shoulder, before feeling in Carl's pockets for the car keys.

She found his driving gloves and his lucky-dip Christmas

gift, but it was an unpleasant shock to discover that there was no sign of the car keys.

When a second, more thorough, search failed to produce them, she bit her lip in vexation. He must have slipped them in his trouser pocket.

But if she went looking for him she risked running into Ross again, and she just couldn't face the thought of that.

Which left only one alternative. She must walk.

No doubt the conditions weren't too good, but if she kept to the main drive, in spite of Janet's misgivings she couldn't possibly come to any harm.

She made her way to the outer door and, trying to look casual, glanced around. To her relief she could no longer see Ross, and no one seemed to be paying her the slightest attention.

Slipping out, she closed the door, pulled up her fur-trimmed hood and, head bent against the driving snow, left the lights of Beinn Mor behind her and set off up the drive.

As she had known quite well, but stubbornly refused to admit even to herself, her clothing and footwear were totally inadequate and her feet were soon icy cold and saturated.

She had been hoping to keep to the broad tyre tracks of the four-wheel drive but the snow had already completely obliterated them.

Slipping and sliding, she tried to stay where the cover of snow was at its thinnest, but even so it was over her shoes, and, more often than not, she was ankle deep.

Though tired, she was young and fit and, in better weather conditions, a mile would have meant nothing to her. But now her jacket and the skirt of her dress were clinging round her wetly, and the wind and snow beating into her face slowed her down and seemed to sap her strength.

After covering what seemed like miles, but in reality could

only have been about half a mile, she veered a little off course and, stumbling over some hidden obstacle, went sprawling.

When she had got her breath back, she struggled unsteadily to her feet and, wielding will-power like a whip, battled on.

But bone-weary, numbed by the intense cold and starting to feel strangely light-headed, she found it almost impossible to steer a straight course.

Weaving about, and falling more and more often, she was forced to battle against a strong desire to lie down in the snow and go to sleep.

She was picking herself up for the umpteenth time when she became aware that there were headlights coming up the drive behind her.

Relief flooded through her, helping to clear her muddled state. No doubt Janet had given Carl her message, and, realizing that he still had the car keys and she must be on foot, he had come after her.

Standing swaying a little, blinded by the headlights, she waited until the big car drew up alongside and Carl jumped out.

Only it wasn't Carl.

'What the devil do you think you're playing at?' Ross demanded, with a kind of raging calm. 'Have you no sense? You're not in a London suburb now. You're in the Cairngorms...'

Bundling her unceremoniously into the big black Range Rover, he stripped off her saturated jacket and replaced it with his own fleece-lined anorak.

It was far too big across the shoulders, and the sleeves came over her hands, but it still held the comforting heat of his body, and that brought such a surge of emotion welling up that she was forced to bite her lip.

Clambering behind the wheel once more, he set off up the

drive, the clash of gears showing only too clearly the extent of his fury.

'It's a blessing Janet noticed that Carl's car was still there. Even then she could hardly believe you'd been *quite* so foolish and spent precious time looking for you, until one of the guests mentioned that she'd seen you slip out. When Janet realized you really *had* gone, and she was unable to locate Carl, she came to find me…

'Damn it, woman,' he berated her, 'haven't you any idea what a risk you were taking?'

'I thought if I kept to the drive—'

He brushed that aside. 'If you'd twisted an ankle, strayed off course, or lost consciousness exposed to temperatures this low without being properly equipped, you'd almost certainly have been dead before any search party could find you…'

Flayed by his quiet fury, she fought back. 'I can't see why you're so angry. As you think so badly of me, why should you care what happens to me?'

'I don't,' he said brutally. 'But if someone is found dead just before Christmas it's bound to cast a blight over both the festivities and the skiing…'

Stricken by that *I don't*, and realizing only too clearly the truth of what he was saying, she whispered, 'I'm sorry.'

But as though she hadn't spoken he went on, 'Added to that, it isn't the kind of publicity Beinn Mor is looking for. But I don't suppose that matters a great deal to someone like you.'

The contempt in his voice did what his angry words had been unable to do, and she was forced to turn her head away so he wouldn't see the tears she could no longer hold back.

But perhaps he sensed that she was crying, because he said no more.

In the ensuing silence, broken only by the shush of the tyres and the click of the windscreen wipers as they cleared the snow, she fought to regain command of her emotions.

Without success.

Since childhood, she had always displayed great self-control and had seldom cried. Even when her parents had died, for Carl's sake she had tried to hide her grief. But now the flood-gates had been opened she was unable to halt the flow of tears.

She found herself crying silently, bitterly, for all the sadness in her life. For the death of her parents, for the loss of her mother's ring, for a failed marriage and for a magical, unexpected attraction that had sprung into life so suddenly and so strongly, only to die. And—perhaps the saddest thing of all—for what might have been.

Then, blurred by her tears, the lights of Dunbar came into view, and a moment later they were pulling up by the side door.

CHAPTER SIX

PURPOSEFULLY, Ross switched off the engine, doused the head-lights and came round to help her out.

The effects of the cold, and a kind of belated shock, had made her start to tremble in every limb as, clutching her bag, the tears still sliding down her cheeks, she climbed out un-steadily.

Her feet were so numb that she was unable to feel them, and she stumbled and would have fallen if he hadn't caught and held her.

With his free hand he opened the door, then, lifting her, cradling her against his chest like a baby, he carried her inside and closed the door behind them with his heel.

She had opened her mouth to tell him that her keys were in her bag, but he went straight past the door to the flat, across the main hall and up that lovely sweep of staircase, reaching the top with no discernible change in his breathing.

A small part of her brain was marvelling at how fit he must be when, turning right, he stopped outside a beautifully carved door.

Stooping a little, he turned the knob without putting her down and carried her into what appeared to be his own private suite.

The sitting room was beautifully furnished with well-chosen

antiques, but a large sheepskin rug and cushioned armchairs drawn up before a blazing fire gave it a cosy appearance.

His bedroom was large and furnished with period pieces and a handsome four-poster.

Finding her voice, she asked through chattering teeth, 'Why have you brought me here?'

Without bothering to answer, he crossed to the door of an en suite bathroom that stood a little ajar and, shouldering it open, strode inside.

Setting her down carefully, and still half supporting her, he tossed aside the handbag she was still clutching and helped her out of the anorak.

When he would have stripped off the rest of her saturated clothing, she made an attempt to push him away and demanded hoarsely, 'What are you doing?'

'Helping to prevent hypothermia.'

Panic making her sound ungracious, she said, 'I can manage. I don't need any help.'

'Let's see, shall we?' He took his arm away and stepped back.

Without his support her knees buckled and she was forced to clutch at the sink.

Catching a glimpse of herself in the mirror, she realized she was a sorry sight. Her clothes were plastered to her, her eyes looked like dark holes in her white, tear-stained face, and her hair had come free from its clip and was hanging round her shoulders in wet rats' tails.

'Well?' he demanded impatiently.

Knowing he wouldn't move until she had made a start, she bent and tugged fruitlessly at one saturated shoe. Bending down made her head swim, and she swayed dangerously.

Muttering something under his breath, he caught her and, stooping, removed both her shoes before taking off her dress.

When he would have stripped off the undies that were clinging round her like a wet shroud, she made an inarticulate protest.

'Don't be stupid,' he said curtly. 'I've seen you naked before and you were quite happy about it.'

'That was different,' she mumbled.

'Different in what way?'

Then they had *both* been naked and drawn together by a wonderful surge of feeling that had raised them to the heights and made everything seem right, destined to happen. But now everything had changed, and it would just be *her* that was naked...

When she remained silent, he said sardonically, 'If you're afraid that if I see you naked I won't be able to keep my hands off you, you don't need to worry. I can assure you that you're quite safe from me.'

His tone made it plain that he wouldn't touch her with a bargepole, and, mortified, she said with pathetic dignity, 'You've made your feelings perfectly clear, and I'd like to do the same. *I don't want your help.* I just want you to leave me alone...'

Losing patience, he said curtly, 'For heaven's sake stop acting like an idiot and let's have you out of those wet things and into a warm shower.'

Brooking no further argument, he stripped off the rest of her sodden clothes and took the clip from her dishevelled hair.

When he'd adjusted the temperature of the shower to just warm, he steered her beneath the flow of water and ordered, 'Hold on to the rail, and stay there until I tell you.'

Holding on as he'd instructed, she closed her eyes and let the comforting warmth seep through her until she ceased shaking, the pins and needles in her hands and feet stopped and her whole body gradually came back to life.

As soon as she reached to turn off the water, the shower door opened and Ross asked, 'All right?'

Without waiting for an answer, he produced a large bath sheet and wrapped it around her.

Utterly drained of energy, with no strength or will-power left to fight, or even think, she stood like a tired child while he rubbed her hair, then dried her, his face aloof, his hands firm but gentle, his touch completely impersonal.

When she was dry and warm and wrapped in a soft towelling bathrobe that was several sizes too big, he produced a bathroom stool for her to sit on while he brushed out her long hair.

Then, leaving it curling damply onto her shoulders, he led her to one of the chairs in front of the living-room fire and settled her into it.

The fire, which had been replenished with split logs, was blazing cheerfully, and like someone in a stupor, she sat gazing into the flames.

As Ross turned away, Onions appeared from seemingly nowhere and jumped onto her knee. Apparently pleased to have found her again, he paddled for a moment or two with velvet paws, then reached to rub his furry face against hers before settling himself in her lap and purring contentedly.

Ross returned and, having rolled up the sleeves of the bathrobe, put a brandy glass into her hand and said, 'Sip that.'

'I don't like brandy,' she protested weakly.

'Whether you like it or not is immaterial. It's for medicinal purposes, so do as I say and drink it.'

Shuddering slightly as the brandy burnt the back of her throat, she muttered, 'I hate bossy men.'

He surprised her by laughing. 'So you haven't lost your spirit.'

But if that had been the case she wouldn't be sitting here taking orders from a man who believed she was a slut and a liar.

She would have insisted on going straight back to the flat she shared with Carl.

Thinking of Carl made her realize that if Janet had told him she'd set off to walk he might be concerned about her...

As though reading her thoughts, Ross said, 'While you were in the shower, to prevent anyone worrying, I talked to Beinn Mor and told them you're safe.'

'Thank you...'

Aware that, when he'd quite possibly saved her life, a mere 'thank you' was inadequate, she added stiltedly, 'It was good of you to leave the party and come after me. I'm really very grateful.'

'Does that mean you're offering to sleep with me to show your gratitude?'

'No, it doesn't!'

'Pity. Not that I would have taken up your offer. Your physical charms seem less alluring since I've discovered what kind of woman you are.'

Putting the glass on the table with a little thump, she lifted Onions down and got to her feet.

'Rushing off?' Ross asked mockingly.

'If Carl's back he'll wonder where I've got to.'

'I'm sure that if he realized just what you're really like he'd look no farther than the nearest man's bed.'

At the end of her tether, and desperate to escape, she made her way unsteadily to the door, Onions at her heels.

Ross got there first and, with a mocking flourish, opened it for her. 'I'll see you safely to the flat.' She was about to argue when, seeing the determined look on his face, she thought better of it, and, her bare feet squeaking a little on the oak flooring, she allowed herself to be escorted.

When they reached the top of the stairs, he took her arm in a firm grip.

Finding his touch unbearable, she tried to shake it off, but he would have none of it. 'Don't be a fool,' he said crisply. 'It would be awful for Carl if you fell down the stairs and broke that beautiful neck.'

His tone indicated that, personally, he wouldn't care one iota.

When they reached the hall he let her go, and, breathing a sigh of relief, she made her way to the flat as quickly as possible.

It wasn't until they reached the door that she realized the key was in her bag, and she'd left that, and her wet clothes, in Ross's bathroom.

The events of the night catching up with her, she felt like bursting into tears.

But, once again reading her thoughts with great accuracy, he said caustically, 'Don't worry, I'll take care of the evidence, and, in the meantime, I have a master key.'

He opened the door and ushered her inside.

There was a little flurry of movement as Onions, who had accompanied them unnoticed, darted through the doorway with her.

'Before you go to bed, it would be a good idea to get yourself something to eat,' Ross suggested.

Though she wasn't in the least hungry, it seemed easier to agree. 'I will.'

'Then I'll say goodnight. Sleep well.' With that mocking injunction, he turned and walked away.

She was thankful Carl hadn't returned. It saved having to make excuses or give explanations.

Going straight through to her room, she took off the robe and pulled on her nightdress, then, having cleaned her teeth, she climbed wearily into bed.

Onions, who had been following her backwards and forwards like a dog, jumped on the bed and snuggled down beside her.

His warm, furry body and his contented purr were strangely

comforting as she recalled Ross's anger and thought about what he had said.

If you'd twisted an ankle, strayed off course, or lost consciousness exposed to temperatures this low without being properly equipped, you'd almost certainly have been dead before any search party could find you...

Thinking back, and recalling her light-headed state and the desire she had felt to lie down in the snow and go to sleep, she knew she must have been close to losing consciousness.

If he hadn't come after her when he did, she might easily have lost her life... Almost before the thought was completed, she was fast asleep.

When she awoke, the room was full of snowy light, and Onions was still curled up beside her, his eyes closed tightly. Only an occasional twitch of his white whiskers disturbed his perfect stillness.

It felt early, and Cathy's inclination was to turn over and go back to sleep. But a glance at the alarm clock by her bed told her that, in reality, it was almost a quarter to ten.

For the second morning running she was going to be seriously late.

The flat was silent, confirming that Carl had already gone, and the knowledge that *she* should be working, too, galvanized her into action.

As she climbed gingerly out of bed so as not to disturb her visitor, she heard the sound of a door closing quietly.

She must have been mistaken in thinking Carl had already gone. Though why was he still here this late?

Pulling on her robe, she went to find out, but there was no one there after all.

Realizing that the sound she had heard must have been Carl leaving, she hurried back to brush her teeth and shower.

She was pleased to find that physically she was back to normal, and suffering no after-effects of her own stupidity.

Of course, if it hadn't been for Ross's swift action it might well have been a different story. Indeed she had a great deal to thank him for, though his unkind taunts and his abrasive manner had made it difficult for her to express her gratitude.

When she was dried and dressed in a fine wool skirt and a cream button-through top, her hair neatly coiled and wearing a touch of make-up to hide any lingering pallor, she went though to the kitchen to make a quick coffee.

Carl's breakfast dishes had been rinsed and turned upside down on the draining board, and a note in his big, sprawling handwriting had been propped against the kettle.

It was very early when I left and you were still sleeping soundly, so I decided not to wake you. At first light Kevin and I are taking a small group off on a winter survival course, which means I'll be away tonight. We're expecting to be back tomorrow, probably late afternoon. Hope you're suffering no ill effects from last night. Honestly, Sis, I thought you had more sense!

With a wry grimace at the rider, Cathy put the kettle on and reached for the instant coffee.

As she did so, a thought occurred to her: if Carl had left very early, she must have been mistaken when she'd thought she had heard a door close. Unless he'd returned for something he'd forgotten?

But that wasn't likely. And if he had, surely he would have stayed to have just a brief word?

She was gulping down the last of the coffee when Onions appeared and came over to wind around her ankles in a morning greeting.

She stooped to rub behind his ears and was rewarded with an appreciative chirrup.

'What about a saucer of milk? Then I must run.'

Ignoring the offer of milk with great disdain, he led the way to the door.

She was all set to close it behind her, when it occurred to her that her keys were in her handbag and she would be unable to get back in again until Ross had returned it.

Deciding not to take any chances, she left the door on the latch and headed for the study, with Onions leading the way, tail erect, like a military escort.

When they reached the main hall, he abandoned her to head towards the kitchen and breakfast.

Opening the study door, she found that the fire was burning brightly, but the room was empty.

She had psyched herself up for the forthcoming meeting with Ross, and it was something of an anticlimax to find that he wasn't there.

A guilty glance at the clock told her it was high time she was at work, but first of all she must phone Beinn Mor and ask if her ring had been found.

Along with her keys, her mobile was in her handbag, so she used the phone on the desk, finding the number programmed in.

Margaret answered and, on hearing Cathy's voice, exclaimed, 'We were so relieved when Ross told us you were safe! Are you feeling all right this morning?'

'I'm fine, thanks to Janet and Ross.'

Apparently not totally convinced, Margaret asked, 'Will you be spending the day in bed?'

'Certainly not. There's absolutely nothing wrong with me. I'm ready to start work. But before I do, there's something I want to ask…'

When she had explained about losing her ring, Margaret was concerned and sympathetic.

'No one has mentioned finding a ring… Any idea where you might have lost it?'

'Not really. The only thing I'm sure of is that I was wearing it when Carl and I left the flat to come to the party.'

'I'm so sorry. It must be very upsetting for you. But now I know it's missing I'll have a thorough search made.'

'I'm sorry to cause you all this trouble.'

'It's no trouble at all. I just pray someone comes across it quickly.'

'Thanks.'

'Try not to worry. The moment it comes to light I'll let you know.'

On that optimistic note, Cathy put the phone down with a sigh. All she could do now was live in hope.

Sitting down behind the desk, she switched on the computer and, dismissing all thoughts of both Ross and the missing ring, prepared to do some work.

She worked steadily throughout the day, stopping only to have a brief lunch of coffee and sandwiches that the young maid brought in, then slipping back to the flat to wash her hands.

This time, her mind on other things, she pulled the door to without thinking, only realizing her mistake when it had clicked shut. Which meant that when she finished work, she would have to find Ross and ask for her bag back.

Throughout the afternoon, apart from pausing to switch on the lights and throw a couple of logs on the fire, Cathy worked non-stop, until a growing stiffness alerted her to the fact that she had sat for too long without moving.

Glancing at the clock, she found it was going up the hill for seven.

She had just finished backing up the day's work when the door suddenly opened, making her jump.

At the sight of Ross, casually elegant in well-cut trousers and a black polo-necked sweater, her heart gave a drunken lurch, then began to race madly.

Though it made no sense, all through the day at the back of her mind had been a longing to see him. But now he was here, with a complete reversal of feeling, she wished she could have escaped back to the flat before he'd appeared.

But of course she needed the keys.

Striding over to the desk, he stood looking down at her, before asking with cool politeness, 'How are you feeling today?'

His nearness unsettled her, but trying her utmost not to let it show, she answered steadily, 'I'm right as rain, thank you.'

'No ill effects?'

She shook her head. 'None.' Then, knowing she owed it to him, she said, 'For which I have you to thank. I believe you saved my life.'

'A dangerous statement.'

When she looked at him blankly, he explained with a little crooked smile, 'There's an old oriental belief that if you save someone's life, from then on they belong to you.'

Guessing he'd only said that to knock her off balance, she retorted lightly, 'Well, as I know you don't want me, I won't worry about it.'

'Suppose I said you were mistaken, and I *do* want you?'

His expression was inscrutable, but she realized that there

was something different about him about the vibes she was picking up.

Though it was almost imperceptible, she was sure that his manner had changed. There was a hidden excitement, a hint of triumph that had put a dangerous gleam in his eye.

'I would know you were only saying that to...' She faltered to a stop.

'Throw you?' he suggested.

Ignoring that, she switched off the computer and rose to her feet.

He didn't move back to give her room, as she had expected, but remained standing so close that she fancied she could feel the heat of his body.

Trapped between his tall, broad-shouldered frame and the desk, she said in a stifled voice, 'If you'll excuse me, I'd like to go back to the flat.'

Without moving an inch, he told her, 'I've got a better idea. As Carl won't be home tonight, we'll have dinner together.'

All her earlier desire to see him, to be with him, had vanished. All she wanted now was to get back to the flat and be alone.

'Thank you, but I need an early night.'

Looking completely unruffled, he pointed out, 'Presumably you'll have to eat before you go to bed.'

'I'll get myself a snack.'

He shook his head. 'I'd much rather you had dinner with me.'

Taking a deep breath, she said with a boldness she was far from feeling, 'Perhaps I should make it quite plain that I don't want to have dinner with you.'

'Perhaps *I* should make it quite plain that that was an order not a suggestion.'

'You can't give me orders about what I do in my own time,' she retorted indignantly.

'Do you want to bet? Apart from the fact that I hold the whip hand, don't forget that now I've saved your life you belong to me.'

'That's a lot of rubbish.'

'Don't be too sure.'

Her heart beating like a drum, she objected, 'As you obviously hate the sight of me, I don't see why you want my company. Unless you're planning to give me a hard time.'

He laughed, white teeth gleaming. 'How clever of you to guess. But that's only part of the evening's...shall we say entertainment?'

Knowing he was trying to frighten her, and unwilling to let him see he was succeeding, she asked with what coolness she could muster, 'So what did you have in mind for the rest?'

'You'll find out in due course.'

She shook her head firmly. 'I'm going straight back to the flat.'

'What will you do if you're unable to get in?' he queried innocently.

With an unpleasant jolt, she recalled that he still had her bag.

Watching her face, and seeing the dawning realization that she was in a cleft stick, he smiled.

'Don't you think it's time to admit defeat?'

Presumably Carl had taken the car over to Beinn Mor and left it there, which meant she was stranded at Dunbar, and she couldn't get into the flat without Ross's co-operation.

'I don't appear to have much choice,' she conceded with what grace she could muster. 'As things are, you seem to hold all the cards.'

'You could always tell me to go to hell,' he suggested with a devilish glint in his eye.

'I *could*,' she agreed slowly. 'But in the circumstances I fail to see what help that would be.'

'Sensible woman,' he applauded. 'Then, as it's all settled, shall we go up?'

'Go up?' she echoed, hanging back.

'To my suite.'

'Can't we eat down here?'

'I usually eat upstairs in front of the fire unless I have guests, and tonight there'll just be the two of us. A *tête-à-tête*, you might say. The kind of thing we enjoyed at Ilithgow House,' he added for good measure.

There was something in his voice, an underlying purpose, a hint of satisfaction, that sounded an alarm bell.

Distrusting his motives, she protested, 'I'd rather eat in the main dining room.'

'I'm afraid that isn't convenient. You see, it's Cook's night off.'

'But if it's the cook's night off, what difference does it make where we eat?'

'Quite a lot, actually. You see *I'll* be cooking.'

'You have a kitchen in your suite?'

'Got it in one.'

Still she held back, playing for time. 'When the whole house belongs to you, I really don't understand why you need a self-contained suite.'

'Strictly speaking, I don't any longer. But I'll tell you all about it over a pre-dinner drink.'

When she still hesitated, he said practically, 'Even if you decide not to stay, you'll need to come up for your handbag.'

The *even if you decide not to stay* seemed to offer her a choice, while common sense told her that that was eyewash. But, seeing nothing else for it, she bowed to the inevitable.

A hand at her waist, he escorted her into the hall and up the stairs. Though his touch was light, it put her in mind of the proverbial iron fist in a velvet glove, and made it clear that he had no intention of being gainsaid.

But he wasn't a man to do anything without a good reason, and she couldn't help but wonder *why* he had acted as he had, *why* he had insisted on her having a meal with him.

Given what he thought of her, it didn't make sense that he wanted her company, and she could only conjecture that it had something to do with the subtle change in his manner she had noticed earlier.

When they reached his suite, opening the door, he stood aside and invited softly, 'Won't you walk into my parlour?'

The little smile that accompanied his cryptic invitation made her blood go cold and a shiver run up and down her spine.

Stopping dead in her tracks, the breath caught in her throat, she looked up at him.

'Something wrong?' he asked, his face innocent.

'You're trying to scare me,' she accused jerkily.

'Now, why should I want to do that?'

To keep her off balance, perhaps? To exact some kind of revenge?

But though she was almost certain that she was right, it seemed too absurd and melodramatic to charge him with any such thing.

When, not sure quite what to say, she said nothing, he lifted a well-marked brow and insisted, 'Well?'

She half shook her head. Though she felt as if she was walking straight into a trap, seeing nothing else for it, she allowed herself to be ushered into his living room.

With an air of subdued triumph that did absolutely nothing to alleviate her apprehension, he closed the door behind her.

Then, indicating one of the armchairs, he asked, 'Won't you sit down?'

At first she sat on the very edge of the chair, back straight, tension in every limb, as though poised for flight.

Hiding a smile, he asked with a bland politeness that grated on her, 'What would you like to drink?'

Noting that smile, and aware that to let him see how nervous she was would be playing into his hands, she sat back and did her utmost to at least *appear* relaxed as she answered, 'A dry sherry, please.'

There were standard lamps burning in the corners of the room, but the main lights were off, and the pools of golden light combined with the flickering firelight made the room cosy and intimate.

Much too intimate.

He poured them both a sherry and, when she had accepted hers, took the chair opposite. Then, his smoke-grey eyes gleaming between thick lashes, he simply sat and looked at her.

Unnerved by that silent scrutiny and wishing, now it was too late, that she had never allowed herself to be coerced into coming up here with him, she tried hard to get a grip.

After all, she asked herself stoutly, what could he actually *do* to her?

He smiled a little, as though once again he knew exactly how she was feeling.

Racking her brains for something to say, Cathy moistened her dry lips and reminded him, 'You were going to tell me how you come to have this suite?'

'So I was…' he agreed smoothly.

Though the mocking glint in his eye made it clear that he knew quite well why she was eager to keep things on a mundane plane, he seemed content to go along with it, at least for the time being.

'The night we met, I believe I mentioned that my parents split up and that my mother went to London to live?'

'Yes.'

'Well, after about a year, to everyone's surprise, my father remarried. My new stepmother and I disliked one another so heartily that I told my father I wanted to go to London and live with my mother. He was very much against me doing any such thing. He'd only agreed to a divorce on condition that I and my sister stayed in Scotland with him. When he realized I was adamant, so that my stepmother and I need have as little contact as possible, he suggested that I make use of the self-contained suite that had been my grandmother's.

'I liked the comparative privacy it provided and the luxury of having my own space, so even when I inherited the house and the estate I decided to keep the suite for my personal use.'

He fell silent, and for a while Cathy sipped her sherry and, avoiding looking at him, stared resolutely into the fire.

But, only too aware that his eyes were on her face, and feeling the sexual tension beginning to tighten, she searched frantically for something to say to keep the conversation going.

Without success.

The only question she could think of to ask was, why had he brought her up here? And she knew he would only answer that in his own good time.

When that silent scrutiny had stretched her nerves almost to breaking point, guessing that that was his intention and unwilling to oblige him, she clenched her teeth and took a fresh grip.

Telling herself firmly that he could only win this war of nerves if she allowed him to—and she would see him in hell first—she looked up and deliberately met and held his gaze.

It took every last ounce of her courage, but it was worth it when the wry amusement in his grey eyes was replaced by a gleam of respect.

Sketching the kind of salute that fencers gave when their

opponent had scored a hit, he uncoiled his long length from the chair and, donning the mask of suave host, said, 'You must be getting hungry. I'll see about dinner.'

She felt a little surge of triumph, and her voice sounded confident even in her own ears as she asked, 'Can I do anything to help?'

He shook his head. 'Everything's prepared...'

It shook her to realize he must have planned this little *tête-à-tête* in advance.

'All you need to do is eat it...'

With a grin that suddenly lightened the atmosphere, he added, 'And perhaps a compliment on my cooking skills wouldn't go amiss.'

Holding on to her advantage, she told him, 'I think I can manage that, so long as you don't plan to poison me.'

A shiver ran through her as he answered silkily, 'I *do* have plans for you, but I can assure you that they don't include poison.'

CHAPTER SEVEN

HAVING effortlessly regained the upper hand, Ross disappeared into the kitchen.

Looking longingly at the door, she considered getting up and walking out. But it would be no use leaving without her keys. However, if she could find her handbag...

Rising cautiously to her feet, all sound muffled by the thick carpet, she set about searching for it.

Standing on the top of a bookcase, a silver-framed photograph of a lovely woman with fair hair and a charming smile, a woman who was no longer young, caught her eye.

There was something about that face that was strangely familiar, as if she had seen it somewhere before. But unable to think where she put it out of her mind and hurriedly continued her search.

There was no sign of the bag in the living room, and, taking a deep breath, she went to look in the bedroom and bathroom.

Finding it in neither, she told herself vexedly that it *had* to be somewhere.

She had returned to the bedroom to search more thoroughly when, glancing up, she froze.

Ross was standing in the open doorway, watching her, one shoulder leaning negligently against the doorjamb.

'Looking for something?' he drawled.

She swallowed. 'My bag.'

'If you'd thought to ask me, I could have told you exactly where it was.'

Stifling the retort that trembled on her lips, she said steadily, 'I'd like to have it, please.'

'Of course,' he agreed, leading the way back to the sitting room. 'If you look alongside the chair you were sitting in…'

It was exactly where he had indicated.

But she was certain it hadn't been there previously. 'Thank you,' she said stiffly.

'My pleasure.' Then, becoming the urbane host once more, he said, 'Now, if you're ready to eat?'

Recognizing that it was too late to make her escape, she reluctantly resumed her seat.

A moment later he wheeled in a dinner trolley set for two and, placing it at a comfortable distance from the fire, brought in a couple of dining chairs.

No doubt due to the stress of the situation, her appetite had once again deserted her, but she obediently took the chair he held for her.

As soon as she was seated he sat down opposite and, having poured white wine into two glasses, raised his in a toast. 'Here's to us.'

His expression gave nothing away, and she was unable to penetrate that unreadable mask. But once again she could sense that change in him, as if something momentous had happened.

Wondering what he was up to, she took a sip of the wine, finding it was light and delicate on her tongue and chilled to perfection.

The simple meal, seafood rolled in crêpes, with a creamy sauce and a crisp side salad, was delicious. It was followed by cheese and fruit and an excellent coffee that, at Ross's suggestion, they moved into the armchairs to drink.

In spite of her initial lack of appetite, and all her misgivings, Cathy had thoroughly enjoyed the meal and said so.

He thanked her gravely. Then, a gleam in his eye, he added, 'Though when it comes to cooking my repertoire is decidedly limited, as in other pursuits I always aim to please.'

Opting to take that somewhat ambiguous remark at face value, she agreed, 'I'm sure you succeed.'

'Of course, the most important thing is to have someone *to* please.'

The deepening gleam of devilment in his eyes made him practically irresistible and warned her she was on dangerous ground.

Gathering herself, she hurriedly changed the subject. 'Earlier I noticed a photograph of a lovely, fair-haired woman on the bookcase...'

'My mother.'

On an impulse, she said, 'Tell me about her. You mentioned that she went to live in London...?'

'Yes. Unfortunately she died several years ago.'

'Oh, I'm sorry. In that case I must be mistaken. I felt sure I knew her face...'

'Perhaps you picked up the strong likeness between her and Marley?'

'Yes, no doubt that was it.'

Something in his expression made her ask, 'You were very fond of her?'

His face softened. 'Yes, very fond. It came as a shock when she died. She was only in her late forties. She married very young. Too young. She was barely eighteen when I was born.

'She and my father were an ill-matched pair, with very little in common. He was a handsome man, but serious and quiet, a bit on the dour side, while she was fun-loving, sunny-natured and a romantic through and through.

'When they first met she already had a steady boyfriend called Toby, but Toby was as pleasant and ordinary and unexciting as the boy next door. Whereas, in her eyes, a Scottish laird who had a house like a small castle was a Mr Rochester-type hero and consequently surrounded by an aura of romance and mystery that was irresistible. Despite the fact that he was almost twenty years older than her, within a few months of meeting they were married, for better or for worse.

'She loved Dunbar on sight and looked all set to be very happy here, but sadly that happiness failed to materialize. Though inside a year she had given birth to the son and heir my father had been hoping for, then three years later to a much-wanted daughter, their relationship wasn't a success.

'For the sake of her children she stayed trapped in a loveless marriage for almost fifteen years. Then on a visit to London to attend an old friend's funeral she met up with Toby, who had never married.

'To cut a long story short, they fell in love all over again, and she asked my father for a divorce. He agreed, on one condition: that he was to have custody of the children.

'Marley, who had always been his favourite, was quite content to stay with him, and, while I wasn't so keen, for my mother's sake I urged her to take that chance of happiness.

'As soon as the divorce went through, she and Toby were married. Though they were ideally suited and very happy together, she badly missed Marley and me. She had always had a love of antiques, so to help fill her days and give her an interest, they bought an antiques shop in Notting Hill...'

Until then, Cathy had been using the conversation simply as a safe way to pass the time until she could say goodnight and escape. But now, her full attention captured, she asked, 'Whereabouts in Notting Hill?'

'Salters Lane.'

'I know the shop!' she exclaimed. 'I went in there once, and I think I met your mother. That's why the photograph was familiar.'

Picking up on her excitement, he suggested, 'Tell me about it.'

'I had to pass the shop on my way to school, and sometimes I stopped to look at the bric-a-brac in the window. They often had really interesting things. Then one day when I was passing, amongst a collection of Victoriana, there was a paperweight snowstorm that I fell in love with. It was a miniature house, standing serene and beautiful in its glass bubble...'

A strange look flitted across Ross's lean face, but all he said was, 'Go on.'

'All the things on display had a price ticket except that. I wanted it so badly, and I still had my sixteenth birthday money to spend, so I went into the shop to ask how much it was. A petite woman with blonde hair and a lovely, gentle face told me very nicely that the snowstorm belonged to her, and it wasn't for sale.

'I thanked her and turned to leave, but she must have realized how bitterly disappointed I was, because she asked me if I'd like to hold it. When I jumped at the chance, she took it out of the window and let me turn it upside down then hold it while we both watched the snow softly falling around the old house. It was quite magical.

'The next time I passed the shop it was gone from the window. But for a long time afterwards I thought of it as "my house".'

After a moment or two she went on, 'Though quite a few years have passed, I've never forgotten it, and my first sight of Dunbar brought it all back. Now I know why.'

Then a shade uncertainly she added, 'Of course, it might *not* be Dunbar. I only saw it once, so I could be mistaken. But it all seems to fit.'

So far Ross, who had been listening intently, had made no comment beyond that terse, 'Go on'. Now he said, 'You're not mistaken. It is Dunbar. As a child, the snowstorm used to fascinate me, and when I asked about it I was told that it had been specially made for my great, great-grandmother.

'According to letters and diaries that have survived, all the Dunbar women seem to have loved the house and lived here happily—apart from my mother, that is. But though she wasn't happy with my father, she still loved Dunbar, and when she left, she took the snowstorm, which had been a gift from my grandmother, with her.'

'How strange,' Cathy breathed.

Ross agreed. 'Whoever said fate works in mysterious ways wasn't far wrong.'

'No,' she said slowly. 'I just feel so—' she sought for a suitable word '—privileged to have met your mother.'

Then, recalling abruptly just what he thought of her, she braced herself for some stinging rejoinder.

But none came, and, glancing his way, she saw that he appeared to be deep in thought.

After a moment, she asked the question that was in her mind. 'What happened to the shop after she died? Did her husband keep it on?'

He shook his head. 'Toby died first. Oddly enough, as if they couldn't bear to be apart, they died within a few weeks of each other. The shop was willed to me, and I asked Toby's elder brother, who was semi-retired and had often helped out there, to run it for me. Which he was very pleased to do.'

There was a drifting silence, broken only by the rustle and crackle of the logs as they burnt through and settled afresh and the comfortable ticking of the grandmother clock that stood in the far corner.

Once again, Ross seemed to have lapsed into thought, his fair head slightly bent, his expression preoccupied as he gazed unseeingly into the flames.

Realizing that, whilst his mind was on other things, it would be a good time to slip away, she felt for her bag.

Then, rising to her feet, like any ordinary polite guest about to leave, she murmured, 'It's time I was getting back. Thank you for a delicious meal.'

He glanced up, instantly alert, but his voice was lazy, posing no threat, as he remarked, 'I'm sure there's no hurry to get back to an empty flat.'

'I'm tired,' she told him, putting her bag on her shoulder and moving as unobtrusively as possible towards the door. 'I'd really like an early night.'

'Well, I'm quite sure that can be arranged.'

Wondering why such an apparently bland statement managed to sound almost like a threat, she stayed on course for the door.

She was aware that he had risen to his feet, as he added with a touch of mockery, 'But don't you agree that nine-thirty is just a *shade* early?'

Ignoring that, she reached to open the door, but, without appearing to hurry, he got there first and neatly blocked her way.

'If you don't mind, I'd like to leave,' she said, and was annoyed to find that she sounded flustered.

When he showed no sign of moving, she repeated jerkily, 'I'd like to leave. I've had dinner with you as you asked, so you've no further reason to keep me. Now I have my keys I can—'

She broke off in confusion as a single fingertip began to stroke her cheek, his light touch making her heart start to race and effectively rooting her to the spot.

'Before you think of rushing off, wouldn't you like to know why I brought you up here?'

As she hesitated, he smiled at her, a white, slightly crooked smile that made her heart turn over, and coaxed, 'Why don't you come back to the fire and sit down? Then eventually—as the old thriller writers were fond of saying—all will be revealed.'

Her resistance vanquished by that smile and the unstudied charm that always affected her so strongly, she allowed herself to be escorted back to the chair she had just vacated.

'Now, as we've decided to have an early night,' he remarked, as though they were an old married couple, 'what about a nightcap? There's a good selection of liqueurs, so shall I choose something?'

'Maybe just a small one.' Her voice was husky.

He poured them a drink each and handed her a glass. 'Try that.'

She sipped obediently and found it was creamy and apparently innocuous.

'Okay?'

'Yes, fine. Thank you.'

He took a seat opposite and put his glass of whisky on the low table. Then, studying her bare hands, he remarked, 'I see you're still not wearing your wedding ring.'

Her voice as level as she could make it, she reminded him, 'I lost it.'

'So you said.'

'And you didn't believe me.'

'Had you been wearing it when we first met, I might have done. But you *weren't*…' Then, with no change in tone, he said, 'Perhaps you'd like to tell me why…'

She half shook her head. 'But it wasn't what you think…'

'Can you *blame* me for thinking you'd taken it off to hide

the fact that you were married? To enable you to have a little "fun" should the opportunity present itself? Well, can you?'

'No,' she admitted in a small voice. 'But it wasn't like that.'

'So why weren't you wearing it?'

'I wish I could explain,' she said helplessly.

'Try.'

'I can't,' she admitted. 'But last night when I told you I'd lost it, it was the truth.'

'Marley certainly believes you. She and Janet have spent a good part of the day searching Beinn Mor, without success.' Then casually he added, 'But I suppose if the ring can't be found Carl will replace it.'

Thinking of the cherished memories she had of seeing her mother wearing it, Cathy shook her head sadly, 'It wouldn't be the same.'

He pounced. 'So, tell me, what makes that particular ring so special?'

Swallowing, she told him the exact truth. 'It has great sentimental value. It means a lot to me.'

'As you could only have been wearing it for a matter of weeks, and you had no hesitation in taking it off when it suited you, you'll have to excuse me if I find that rather hard to believe.'

'No matter what you believe, it *does* mean a lot to me,' she repeated stubbornly.

'Was it engraved?'

'Yes, it was.'

'So, what *was* the engraving?'

'W-what?' she stammered.

With exaggerated patience, he repeated the question.

'Just initials entwined in a love knot.'

'Yours and Carl's?'

Trapped, she said, 'Of course.'

'Anything else?'

'The word *always*.'

'How very romantic.'

'It *was* romantic,' she flared. Then, suddenly feeling a bitter desolation, a certainty that the ring was gone for ever, her eyes filled with tears.

Her distress hit him like a blow over the heart, and, despite the anger he still felt at her refusal to tell him the truth, he regretted pushing her so hard. As she stared into the fire, trying desperately not to let the tears fall, he leaned forward and, taking her left hand, which was clenched into a fist, he straightened and kissed each finger one at a time, before sliding a wide band of chased gold onto her wedding finger.

Surprise made her blink and, as twin tears rolled down her face in tracks of shiny wetness, through a watery haze she found herself looking down at the ring she had just despaired of ever seeing again.

The rush of relief made her cry in earnest, and when Ross lifted her and settled her on his knee she was incapable of protest.

Cradled against him, she struggled for control, but somehow the comfort he was offering only made the tears flow faster.

When she was all cried out, he produced a folded hankie and with a muffled, 'Thank you,' she dried her wet cheeks before handing it back.

He seemed content to hold her, and she wanted to stay where she was, wanted the comfort of his arms, but a kind of perverse pride made her struggle off his knee and resume her seat.

As soon as her voice was steady enough, she asked, 'Where did you find it?'

'Iain Mackay, one of the estate workers who lives in the village, brought it to me late this afternoon. It was Iain who, in the guise of Father Christmas, was running the lucky dip.

'I'd told him that should there be any presents left over he could take them home to give to his family. He did that and found the ring at the bottom of the sack. Presumably it slipped off when you had your lucky dip.'

'I can't thank him enough for returning it,' she said in a heartfelt voice. 'Does your sister know it's been found?'

'Yes, I rang to tell her. Both she and Janet were delighted.'

'That's nice of them.'

Though touched by her glowing face, he hardened his heart and returned to the attack.

'You'll have to be careful not to lose it again.'

'Yes.'

Reaching out, he took her hand and moved the ring round and round between his thumb and forefinger, before remarking, 'It's so loose it's a miracle it hasn't slipped off before. It might be a good idea to get it made smaller.'

'I wouldn't want to—' About to say, *have it altered*, she stopped abruptly and changed it to, 'I wouldn't want to lose it again, so I'll take your advice. In the meantime I'll wrap some wool or cotton round it.'

'How did you come to buy something that was obviously the wrong size?'

Weakly she said, 'I happened to like that particular ring.'

He made no comment, and she was breathing a sigh of relief when he observed, 'You don't wear an engagement ring?'

'I've never had one.'

'Why was that?'

Thinking of Neil, she said, 'We were only engaged a short time before getting married.'

'I would have thought that someone who—according to Carl—has a romantic streak a mile wide would have liked an engagement ring.'

'I would have liked one. But when we got engaged we didn't have much money.' That, too, was true.

He made no further comment, and she was just trying to assure herself that she was out of the wood, when he said casually, 'There's a couple of things that don't add up.'

'Oh?'

'How do you account for the fact that the edge of your wedding ring is slightly worn, as though for a number of years another ring had rubbed against it? And, secondly, the initials engraved inside aren't C and C, as one might expect, but A and D?'

With no option but to tell the truth, she admitted, 'The initials are A and D because the ring belonged to my mother. Her name was Anne and my father's name was David.'

Keeping her voice flat, dispassionate, she went on, 'When they fell in love and agreed to marry, he bought her a matching pair of rings which she wore for twenty years. After the plane crash that killed them both, her wedding ring was amongst the few personal possessions that were returned to us, but her engagement ring was never found.'

'I see,' Ross said slowly. 'That explains why the ring means so much to you.'

Then, like a cobra striking, he said, 'Why didn't you tell me straight away that it was your mother's? Why pretend the initials inside were yours and Carl's?'

Something inside snapped, and she cried, 'I'm tired of being interrogated and I absolutely refuse to answer any more questions.'

Having slotted all the pieces of the puzzle into place, he already *knew* why, but he'd wanted to hear her admit it.

From the start things hadn't added up, and the hesitant answers she had given when he'd questioned her about her marriage, coupled with Carl's brotherly attitude towards her, had aroused his suspicions and prompted him to do some checking.

When the results had amply confirmed his suspicions, relief had flooded through him.

Hard on the heels of that relief had come anger. Though in a way he was forced to admire her loyalty, he was angry that she'd lied to him, furious to think of all the pain she had caused him.

Determined to make her confess the truth, he had pushed her hard. But though in some ways she appeared fragile, yielding, she had a strength of character that, vexed as he was, he could only appreciate.

And though he knew—couldn't fail to know—how strongly she was attracted to him, perhaps due in part to his previous failed relationship he wouldn't be happy until she had surrendered herself completely, until she was *his*, heart, mind, body and soul. And willing to admit it.

It would mean pushing her even harder, but only that admission, freely given, would compensate for all she had put him through.

And only then could he tell her how very much she meant to him…

After her bold words she had braced herself for a further onslaught, but when he merely sat gazing at her, a strange, preoccupied look on his handsome face, she jumped to her feet and announced shakily, 'I'd like to leave now.'

He uncoiled his long length in one graceful movement and stood looking down at her. 'What's the hurry? It isn't as if your husband will be waiting for you.'

'Please, Ross, let me go.'

She thought his face softened for an instant, but, ignoring her plea, he pressed her gently back into her chair.

'I don't know what you *want*,' she said helplessly. 'I've had dinner with you, I've done everything you asked me to do...'

'Why do you suppose I brought you up here?'

'I don't know.'

He tossed fresh logs onto the fire, before saying, 'I'm sure you do, if you think about it.'

She felt too weary to think, but still she tried.

'Well?'

'Because of the ring?' she hazarded. 'Like a showman, you wanted to stage-manage its return.'

He looked amused. 'Try again.'

The only other thing she could think of was the little scene that had ensued when she had thanked him for saving her life. The strange, lopsided little smile on his face as he'd told her, 'There's an old oriental belief that if you save another person's life, from then on they belong to you.'

And her own light retort, 'Well, as I know you don't want me, I won't worry about it.'

Then his rejoinder which, just momentarily, had shaken her rigid, 'Suppose I said you were mistaken, that I *do* want you?'

But he couldn't have meant it. Certainly not in the literal sense.

As she half shook her head, he observed, yet again reading her thoughts with devastating accuracy, 'You didn't think I meant it?'

Baldly she said, 'No.'

'Why not?'

'Because you'd already made it clear that you wouldn't touch me with a bargepole.'

'I might just have changed my mind.'

Agitation brought her to her feet. 'I don't believe it.'

'Try.'

As she turned away he came over and, holding her upper arms lightly, touched his lips to the warmth of her nape, scattering her wits and making her heart thump against her ribs.

Telling herself that this was just another of his games, she stood still as a statue, her teeth clenched, while he brushed her silky top aside so that his mouth could explore the side of her neck and the smooth skin of her shoulder.

'Don't!' Unable to stand any more, she jerked away.

But, drawing her back against him, he bent his head to put his cheek against hers. 'There's no need to pretend,' he told her softly. 'I already know what kind of woman you are.'

She played the only card she held. 'A married one.'

One arm holding her, his free hand beneath her chin, he tilted her head back on his shoulder.

For a helpless moment she glimpsed his strong face, intriguingly inverted, before she was forced to close her eyes.

As his lips explored her exposed throat and the pure line of her jaw, he observed softly, 'Being married has never held you back before.'

Swallowing, she tried to ignore the havoc his kisses were creating as she reminded him, 'Yesterday you told me that you never got involved with married women, that you hated the idea of having slept with an employee's wife.'

'That was yesterday morning. But last night, when I saw you flirting first with Robert and then with Cunningham, and realized that even with your husband close at hand being married meant nothing to you, I decided I was being overscrupulous. I might as well have my share of what was on offer.'

Rage lending her strength, she wrenched herself free and turned on him like a fury.

'Absolutely *nothing* was "on offer", as you so insultingly put it. And as for you "having your share", if you were the last man on earth I wouldn't give you so much as a kiss under the mistletoe.'

He laughed, adding to her fury. 'Believe me, I intend to have a great deal more than that.'

'Or what?'

He shrugged. 'Or I might be tempted to tell your husband just what kind of woman he's married to. Would he be comfortable staying on here if he knew what had happened at Ilithgow House?'

Her heart sank. Suppose Ross did tell him? Carl knew her well enough to be certain that she would never have gone to bed with a man who hadn't been very special. So for her sake he might throw everything away by admitting that his 'marriage' was just a sham.

And it would all be for nothing. It would simply be robbing him of *his* happiness when it was too late to save *hers*.

For a moment she wavered. Dared she chance it?

But Ross wouldn't tell him. She had never been more certain of anything in her whole life.

Studying her changing expressions, as if he were following her train of thought, he asked, 'Well? Have you decided?'

She gave him a steady look and said clearly, 'Yes. You can tell him and be damned.'

Showing no sign of annoyance, he asked, 'You don't think you're taking a risk?'

'No.'

'Why not?'

'Because I don't believe you'd tell him. You're not that kind of man.'

With a wry grin, he admitted, 'I must confess I would have been more than a little concerned if you *had* believed me.'

'So, can I go now?'

He laughed and, taking her upper arms, drew her against him. 'My love, you've only won that particular battle, not the war. I mean to have you in my bed tonight...'

Badly shaken by that careless endearment, and the quiet certainty of that *I mean to have you in my bed tonight*, she tried to tell herself he didn't mean it. He was just trying to frighten her. He wasn't the kind of man who would deliberately seduce another man's wife.

But, though she was almost convinced of that, he appeared to be deadly serious.

While she could already feel her blood beginning to flow faster through her veins, she knew if she was weak enough to allow it to happen she would go down even further in his estimation...

Pulling herself free, she said sharply, 'I've absolutely no intention of sleeping with you.'

'If you would allow me to finish,' he objected mildly, 'I was about to say, "whatever it takes to get you there".'

She couldn't win by physical strength, so she would have to win the war of words. 'It would take anaesthetic,' she assured him sweetly.

'As I like my partner to be wide awake, I've already discounted that.'

'Then the only alternative is taking me against my will.'

He shook his head. 'An unpleasant and unnecessary thought. As well as wide awake, I like my partner to be eager or, at the very least, willing.'

'As I'm neither willing nor eager, I'm afraid you've run out of options.'

'Oh, I wouldn't say that. You've left out the nicest by far. A little friendly persuasion.'

She saw how his grey eyes glittered as he added in a seductive whisper, 'I don't think it will take too long to make you want me.'

He was so sure of himself. But perhaps, considering how quickly she had responded to him that first time, he had every right to be?

A quiver of apprehension running through her, she clung to one thought—if she gave in to him this time, it would merely underline his certainty that she was a slut. Provide him with more opportunities to hurt and humiliate her.

She shuddered.

But in all justice, if she had been hurt and humiliated, it was her own fault.

He wasn't normally a cruel man, she was convinced, and it was her own actions that had made him disillusioned and angry enough to *want* to hurt and humiliate her.

CHAPTER EIGHT

His eyes fixed on Cathy, noting her absolute stillness, watching the changing expressions flit across her face, Ross asked silkily, 'So what do *you* think?'

'I think you're just trying to scare me. I don't believe you're the kind of man who would try to seduce another man's wife.'

'And normally you would be quite right. But this time the circumstances are somewhat exceptional, wouldn't you say? After all, there can't be many wives, especially brand-new ones, who would have been so willing, not to say *eager*, to jump into bed with another man...'

It always came back to that.

She felt a sense of despair.

Drawing her close once more, he said softly in her ear, 'Don't look so unhappy. Once you've got over this sudden unexpected attack of conscience, I'm sure you'll enjoy the whole thing...'

His lips began to wander down the side of her neck, sending little shivers running through her.

Head bent, chin tucked in to deny him access to her slender throat, she tried to marshal her pitifully few defences.

The only way she could emerge unscathed from this planned seduction would be if she could hold out against him.

So somehow she *must*.

But it wasn't going to be easy while her will-power was being undermined by the demands of the flesh. He'd barely touched her, and already her heart was racing and every nerve-ending in her body had zinged into life.

And he knew it.

Softly he said, 'I've been waiting all evening to do this.' With a smooth, commanding movement, he lifted her chin and kissed her mouth.

His lips were firm and warm, and he kept them closed, making it relatively easy for her to remain passive. Even so, the kiss—which lasted no more than ten seconds—made her long to kiss him back.

Just before he lifted his head, taking her by surprise, the tip of his tongue stroked across her mouth, parting her lips and finding the smooth, sensitive inner skin.

Unconsciously, her own pink tongue-tip followed the path of his, moistening lips that suddenly felt dry.

Firelight flickered beguilingly across her cheeks and forehead, and his eyes darkened as he stroked the hollow beneath her lower lip with his thumb.

She caught her breath, suddenly realizing that this was going to be no short, sharp assault on her senses, but a leisurely seduction that would be even harder to hold out against.

With one arm imprisoning her, and the fingers of his other hand tracing the lovely curve of her cheek, he queried, 'So what are you planning to tell Carl when he asks how you spent the evening?'

Deciding it was probably safer to keep talking, she answered, 'I won't need to tell him anything. He won't ask.'

His fingers moving caressingly along her jawline, he persisted, 'But suppose he does? You've been kissed, and not just under the mistletoe. Will you lie about that?'

'There'll be no reason to lie… He'll have no reason to ask,' she insisted breathlessly.

And it was quite true. Knowing Carl, she suspected he would be much too full of his own adventure to wonder how she had spent her time.

'How very trusting of him.'

'Carl isn't the jealous type.' As soon as the words were out, she wished them unspoken.

Ross grinned and, letting his hand slip down to cup her breast, murmured, 'Which in the circumstances is just as well.'

'Please, Ross, don't,' she whispered, trying to push his hand away and failing.

'Why not? It isn't something new. I've held you like this before.'

'But then it was—'

'It was what?'

She half shook her head.

'Tell me, how *did* you regard it? Just as a casual encounter? Two strangers indulging what is no more than an appetite, like any other?'

'No!' she cried. 'It wasn't like that. It wasn't!'

'So what was it like?'

Special…magical…unforgettable… But she could hardly tell him that.

'It was a mistake,' she whispered. 'A mistake I have no intention of repeating.'

'Because you love Carl and don't want to lose him?' Ross asked cynically.

It was her self-respect she didn't want to lose, but how he would jeer if she told him that.

'You *do* love him?' he pursued.

'Yes, I love him very much,' she answered.

'But clearly not enough to make you stay faithful.'

While he spoke, he turned her so that her back was against his broad chest and, one arm holding her against him, he used his free hand to unfasten her heavy coil of hair.

As it tumbled down her back, he slid his hands beneath her silky top to cup both her breasts in his palms and caress them gently.

She could feel the warmth of his fingers through the delicate material of her low-cut bra, and she found herself shivering in anticipation.

But he carefully avoided her nipples, and she waited breathlessly, the aching need to have him touch her growing.

Suddenly realizing how he was starting to seduce her mind as well as her body, she tried to deny that need and remain unmoved.

But she heard his soft laugh and realized that he knew exactly what he was doing to her and how she was feeling.

When he let his hands slide over her ribs and down to her slender waist she gave a little sigh.

It was a sigh of relief, she told herself hastily, but, whatever it was, it changed to a gasp as he deftly unfastened her skirt.

Feeling it begin to slide down her silk-clad legs, she grasped at it, but he caught her hands and held them away.

As it fell round her feet, he began to undo the covered buttons of her cream top.

She knew she should try to stop him, but she was distracted by the way his mouth was moving down the side of her neck to the tender junction where her neck met her shoulder.

An instant later, in one easy movement, he had opened her top and, slipping her arms free of it, sent it to join her skirt.

Ignoring her hoarse protest, he unclipped her bra and tossed it aside, leaving her naked apart from delicate briefs and fine silk stockings.

With an appreciative murmur, he moved her fall of sun-streaked hair to one side and allowed his lips to graze over her nape. Then, taking her by surprise, he nipped at a tendon in her bare shoulder, making her jerk and give an involuntary shudder.

A moment later his hand was following the slim length of one leg down as far as her knee and then back again.

Before she could catch her breath, he was doing the same to her other leg. But this time when his fingers reached the top of her thigh, they slipped beneath the lacy edge of her briefs.

A sensual precursor of the delights to come.

While she stood as though mesmerized, he began to slide her briefs down over her hips, and in the blink of an eye they joined the puddle of discarded clothes at her feet.

With an easy strength he lifted her enough to allow him to kick the offending clothing to one side. Then, as though coming home, his hands returned to the soft curves of her breasts and he lightly trapped the nipples between his fingers, feeling them firm to his touch.

She wanted to turn to him, to put her arms around his neck and press herself against him, to—

Abruptly she snapped off the thought and made an effort to rally her pitifully few defences. If she didn't stop him now, this instant, in a very short time it would be too late.

And when he had had his way he would feel nothing but contempt for her.

Feeling her stiffen, he attacked from another angle. Turning her towards him, he tilted her face up to his. Then he kissed her with a passion that fired her blood afresh, urging her lips to part, and he deepened the kiss until her head started to spin and she had to clutch at him for support.

Then, her feet neatly hooked from beneath her, she found herself lying on the thick sheepskin rug in front of the fire, the leaping flames warming her limbs and gilding her skin with gold.

Stretching out beside her, he let his hands wander caressingly over her, reacquainting himself with the beguiling contours of her body.

Almost dazed with longing, she made no protest as he traced the swell of her breast, the slender waist, the flat stomach and the flare of her hips.

When he reached her legs, he peeled off the silk stockings, leaving her totally naked. Then, bending his head, he took one erect nipple in his warm, wet mouth and suckled sweetly.

Interpreting her strangled gasp correctly, he began to tease the other between his thumb and forefinger, arousing the most exquisite feelings—fierce darts of pleasure that went shooting down to meet the growing heat and urgency between her thighs.

Lost and mindless now, she made a soft sound in her throat, almost like a plea.

He responded by running his free hand down to the nest of pale silky curls and using his long, lean fingers to delicately probe and explore.

When those explorations took on a rhythm that had her moaning and lifting her hips, he stopped and, as if to emphasize his complete mastery, told her, 'As I don't know how long it might be before I'm able to make love to you again, I intend to make the most of tonight.'

While she lay with closed eyes, he swiftly stripped off his clothes before stretching out beside her once more. Kissing her mouth, he whispered, 'If I do anything you don't like, stop me.'

But with her whole being crying out for the release that only he could give her there was no way she could have stopped him.

Murmuring how beautiful she was, and how much he wanted her, and displaying a skill and expertise that showed how well he knew the feminine libido, he pleasured her—finding erogenous zones she had never even dreamt of.

His hands gentle, but relentless, he turned her over and kissed his way from the nape of her neck down her spine to her legs, finding unerringly the vulnerable spots at the base of her spine and behind her knees, and forcing responses that made her a trembling mass of desire.

Then, turning her over once more, he lifted her hips. When she felt the warm wetness of his mouth and tongue, she cried out.

It was like nothing she had ever experienced before, and the pleasure became almost frightening in its intensity, in the feeling it engendered, in its power to stimulate. As his tongue stroked her to the brink of climax she was racked by sensations so exquisite that she thought she might faint.

But even that was nothing compared to the moment when he tipped her over the edge into a whirlpool of feeling, forcing soft moans and cries from her and leaving her limp and quivering.

When she felt him lower himself into the cradle of her hips, thinking herself sated, she was startled as the ecstasy that had started to fade rekindled and reintensified, so that she was once more caught up and carried along by that driving need.

This time they reached the brink in unison, and together were tossed into the maelstrom.

After a little while the intensity of their shared climax gradually passed and their breathing and heart rate began to return to normal.

She became aware of the weight of his fair head on her breast and, love for him filling her entire being, cradled it to her with an almost maternal tenderness.

She was nearly asleep before he moved out of her loosened embrace, and only vaguely aware when, lifting her in his arms, he carried her through to the bedroom and tucked her up in the four-poster.

* * *

When she awoke, just for a split second her mind was a blank, then the sluice gates of memory opened and the events of the evening came flooding back.

Her heart starting to race, she turned her head, only to find she was alone in the big bed. But the dented pillow and the rumpled sheets made it clear that Ross had slept by her side.

Though physically she felt fine, her body sleek and satisfied, mentally she was weighed down with a kind of dull despair that she had let it happen.

What must he think of her?

Why was she even asking herself that? She knew only too well what he must think of her.

What she didn't know was what had made him act in the way he had. Though he had obviously *wanted* her, he was a man who didn't lack self-control...

But of course it was nothing to do with self-control. Last night had been no sudden impulse, but a planned strategy. He had known that Carl would be away and had taken full advantage of the fact to seduce her.

But that didn't add up. She had put him down as a decent man, a man with principles. Had she been completely wrong about him?

The answer seemed to be that she had. That she had made the same mistake about him as she had made about Neil.

But some sure instinct told her that that wasn't so. That no matter how it *looked*, Ross *was* a man with principles.

So why had he gone against those principles? Had it merely been to prove that *she* had no morals?

No... That was too cold-blooded by far.

Though he was a self-controlled, sophisticated man, his behaviour had been more like a primitive man's response to discovering the woman he regarded as *his* had strayed.

In days gone by, no doubt he would have beaten her before

taking her to bed to reassert his ownership. But in these modern times, though feelings might be just as primitive and passionate, it was no longer permissible to beat your woman or use caveman tactics.

But she couldn't really accuse him of using caveman tactics. Though he'd been both arrogant and masterful in the way he had made her body his, he had shunned force and gone for persuasion.

But was that only because he thought she was wanton, and would be a push-over?

As she had been.

With a heart like lead, she recalled his words—words that were printed indelibly on her brain. *I decided I was being over-scrupulous, that I might as well have my share of what was on offer.*

It was quite evident that, though he might *want* her, he still considered her promiscuous and despised her accordingly.

Yet last night she seemed to recall that after putting her in bed he had kissed her gently.

Or had she just imagined that kiss, that sweet display of tenderness?

No, surely not. Though her eyes had been closed, and she had been almost asleep, she could remember how his thistledown kiss had felt. How, light as it was, it had stirred her very soul.

For a moment or two she closed her eyes to try and recapture the feeling.

But she couldn't, and that made her doubt that it had ever happened. Perhaps her imagination had invented the whole thing simply because she had wanted it so very much...

Sighing, she made an effort to push any regrets to the back of her mind. What was done couldn't be altered. The only course open to her now was to carry on as best she could.

Or simply pack her bags and leave.

But if she left she'd have no home, no job and nowhere to go. That in itself wasn't insurmountable, but Carl would want to know *why*. And what could she possibly tell him?

Certainly not the truth. Or *he* wouldn't stay.

It seemed that she would have to stick it out at least until she could think up some story that would satisfy him and enable him to keep his job here without worrying about her.

In the meantime she would have to face a triumphant Ross. Though she dreaded the thought, she was forced to admit that he had every right to be triumphant.

Usually a silent lover, she recalled with shame the moans and cries he had forced from her. Had he needed any further proof of his complete mastery of her body, she had certainly provided it.

With another sigh, she looked at the clock and was shocked to see what time it was. Almost half past nine, and she was still naked and in his bed.

No doubt he had been up and working for an hour or more, and she should be working, too.

Scrambling out of bed, she hurried into the bathroom. The clean, fresh scent of shower gel and a fine spattering of water droplets on the glass confirmed that Ross had already showered and gone on his way.

Standing beneath the flow of hot water, she thought of the night before last, when she had done the same. Then, though he had dried her naked body, his touch, indeed his whole manner, had been as impersonal, as free from any trace of sexual awareness, as it was possible to be.

So what had sparked off the difference?

Once again she found herself struggling with the inexplicable. When she had dried herself and borrowed a spare toothbrush to clean her teeth, with a towel wrapped around her sarong-like, the loose end tucked between her breasts, she went to look for her clothes.

They had been picked up and folded neatly over a bedroom chair. Though she disliked the thought of wearing undies she had worn the previous day, having little choice, she started to pull them on.

Only to find they *weren't* yesterday's undies, but fresh ones that must have been taken from her drawer. The blouse, too, was fresh, as were the stockings, and the skirt had been replaced by slimline trousers and a matching jerkin.

Looking at them blankly, she wondered how they had got there. Had Ross asked a maid to fetch them? Or had he fetched them himself?

It would be very embarrassing if he'd left it to one of the maids...

But it would be even worse if he'd fetched them himself. If he *had*, he would know that she and Carl slept in separate bedrooms.

She tried to tell herself that a lot of married couples must sleep apart, but she couldn't for a moment see Ross swallowing that.

Having dressed as quickly as possible, she had turned to look for the clasp that held her coil of hair in place, when the door between the bedroom and the living room suddenly opened, and Ross appeared in the doorway.

Newly shaven, his clear blue-grey eyes sparkling, his thick corn-coloured hair parted on the left and neatly brushed, he looked fresh and virile and dangerously handsome.

He was dressed with throwaway elegance in dark trousers and a blue silk shirt, open at the neck. The sleeves had been rolled up to his elbows, exposing muscular arms lightly sprinkled with golden hairs. A clean tea towel was knotted casually around his lean hips.

'Good morning,' he said easily. 'Lost something?'

Completely thrown by his sudden appearance, she stammered, 'I—I was just looking for my clip so I could put my hair up.'

'Leave it as it is,' he ordered crisply. 'I like it better loose. It makes you look innocently seductive—as if you're just about to make love.'

Those few words, and the lazily appreciative glance that travelled over her from head to toe, caused heat to run through her veins and her face to fill with burning colour.

Though he couldn't possibly have missed that fiery blush he made no comment about it, nor about her change of clothing, and, scared of rocking the boat, she said nothing.

'I was rather hoping you'd be awake by now,' he went on. 'Breakfast is ready and waiting, and scrambled eggs are best eaten fresh from the pan.'

Both his voice and his manner were relaxed, laid-back, as if nothing out of the ordinary had happened, as if it were the norm for her to wake up in his bed and for them to have breakfast together.

But beneath that civilized veneer ran a current of triumph, the almost savage satisfaction of a conqueror who had fought and won a victory—who had achieved his goal.

He held open the door for her, and, after the briefest of hesitations, she followed him through the living room and into the white-walled, black-beamed kitchen. It lay at the rear of the house, and three long, leaded windows looked out onto a snow-covered landscape.

Though it appeared to be equipped with every modern convenience, the kitchen was attractive and homely, with old oak furniture and an inglenook fireplace, in which a log fire blazed.

Onions had settled himself in front of the fire, white paws curled neatly inwards, and was blinking sleepily at the flames.

Having lifted his head to identify the newcomer, he came over to greet her, chirruping contentedly when she stooped to pet him.

As soon as she was seated at the table, he jumped up and settled himself on her lap.

'Oh, no, you don't,' Ross said. 'You know perfectly well you're not allowed at the table.'

His dignity ruffled, Onions stalked away and jumped onto one of the wide windowsills, where he sat with his back half turned towards them.

With a slight grin, Ross observed, 'Because you were here he thought he could get away with it.'

Having poured freshly squeezed orange juice into two glasses, he dished up breakfast—crispy curls of bacon, tiny button mushrooms and light, fluffy scrambled eggs.

Though Cathy could have sworn she wouldn't be able to eat a thing, after the first mouthful she found she was enjoying it.

For his part, Ross seemed contented with the silence, and, as she could think of nothing to say, they ate without a word being spoken.

When their plates were empty, he dropped them into the dishwasher before asking, 'Would you care for some toast and marmalade?'

She shook her head. 'No, thank you.' Then, like a polite guest, she said, 'That was most enjoyable.'

'It's nice of you to say so,' he told her with mock gravity, adding, 'Coffee or tea?'

'Coffee, please.'

Reaching for the cafetière, he indicated two comfortable-looking chairs standing on a colourful, country-style pegged rug and suggested, 'Let's have it by the fire, shall we?'

As she moved past the windows to sit where he'd indicated, a row of icicles hanging from the eaves caught her eye, and she paused to look out over a snow-covered garden to a lacy coppice.

Somehow, in contrast to the cosy warmth of the room and the leaping fire, the picture-postcard scene appeared even more like a winter wonderland.

The sun shone from a sky of Mediterranean blue, making the icicles sparkle like diamonds and putting a dazzling sugar-frosting on the trees and bushes. In the distance a backdrop of snowy foothills ringed by taller mountains completed a scene so beautiful that it almost brought tears to her eyes.

Onions, who was still sitting on the windowsill, the low sunshine gilding him and turning his luxuriant whiskers into gold wires, looked up at her and, when she rubbed behind his ears, jumped down and followed her back to the fire.

When they were drinking their coffee, Ross, who had been watching her as she looked at the view, asked, 'I take it you like it here?'

'Yes, I do,' she said sincerely. 'It's absolutely beautiful.'

'But you would prefer to live in London?'

'No, not at all. Though London is a wonderfully exciting city, I'd much sooner live in the country. After our parents died we considered moving back to the small country market town where we'd been born.

'But I needed a job that paid well, and the opportunities there were a lot less. Added to that, C—' She broke off abruptly, then, trying not to appear flustered, went on, 'My brother was still at school and hoping to train as a physiotherapist, so it wasn't a good time to be uprooting him.'

'What's your brother's name?' Ross asked casually.

Starting to know how quick he was at picking things up, she was half prepared for the question and, without any perceptible hesitation, answered, 'Cadell.'

'An unusual name,' Ross said smoothly.

It was Carl's middle name, and, feeling on reasonably firm ground, she said truthfully, 'He was named after our paternal grandfather.'

'I see. Tell me, what's your brother like? Does he resemble you in any way?'

Anxious not to tell him too much, she answered, 'No, not really. He takes after our father in looks, while I'm more like our mother.'

'You once told me that you and your brother had been living in the flat your parents had rented.'

'Yes.'

'What happened after you got married?'

'W-what happened?'

'Yes. Where did you live?'

'In the same flat.'

'You and your husband and your brother?'

'Yes,' she answered levelly.

'You told me you let the flat go when you and Carl came up here?'

'Yes.'

'So what happened to your brother?'

'He moved out.'

'Where is he living now?'

'He…he's living with a friend.'

Then intent on escaping any further questions, she rose to her feet. 'It's about time I went downstairs and started work.'

Taking her by surprise, he announced, 'As it's Christmas Eve, I wasn't planning on working today.'

With a feeling of relief, she said, 'Oh... Well, as I know there's a lot to be done, I'm quite happy to carry on alone.'

'I wasn't intending you to work either.'

'In that case I'll go back to the flat and—'

He shook his head decidedly and, his voice becoming intimate, charged with innuendo, he told her softly, 'But I was hoping to make use of your services.'

Agitation making her voice sound shrill, she burst out, 'If you mean what I think you mean—'

Raising a mocking brow, he queried, 'What do you think I mean?'

'You know perfectly well.'

When he merely looked at her, she said hoarsely, 'If you expect me to go to bed with you whenever it suits you...'

'That's exactly what I expect.'

She couldn't bear the thought of just being used and knew she should hate Ross for treating her that way. But though she felt angry and hurt and resentful, she couldn't bring herself to hate him.

Biting her lip until she tasted blood, she cried, 'No, I won't do it. I'll see you in hell before I'll let you use me like that.'

'Bold words,' he said. 'But if you want your husband to keep his job you don't have any choice, my sweet wanton. And it's not as if I'm asking you to do anything you haven't willingly done before...

'However, as it happens, at the moment you're getting all worked up for nothing. What I had in mind for today doesn't involve taking off your clothes.'

'What *does* it involve?' she demanded shakily.

His head tilted slightly to one side, he pretended to consider. 'A little friendly co-operation... I think the worst thing that could happen to you might be a kiss under the mistletoe.'

Knowing he was playing with her, she said sharply, 'Will you please come to the point?'

He rose lithely to his feet. 'The point is, as tonight is the Christmas Eve Ball, I thought we might put the finishing touches to the hall and decorate the tree...'

Annoyed that he had deliberately trailed his coat, but at the same time relieved that she had jumped to the wrong conclusion, she bit her lip.

'Mathersons, the catering firm I've hired, would have seen to it all,' he went on, 'but it's more fun to do a part of it ourselves, wouldn't you agree?'

If she said she didn't want to help, would he just let her go back to the flat and leave her alone?

She very much doubted it.

And if for a short time she could put all the worries and problems that beset her out of her mind and help to decorate the hall of 'her' house, it was a pleasure she didn't want to forego.

But, after all that had happened between them, would co-operating with him on a friendly basis work?

Perhaps it was up to her to make it...

Watching her face, he said, 'Of course, if you really don't want to help...'

Making up her mind, she said, 'I'd like to. I've always loved Christmas and putting up decorations.'

He smiled at her, the coldness and hardness sloughing off like a shed skin, to be replaced with warmth and enthusiasm. 'Come on, then.'

CHAPTER NINE

TAKING her hand, he pulled her to her feet. 'Mathersons were due to make a start at eight o'clock this morning, so shall we see how far they've got?'

Responding to the change in him, her spirits soared, and for the first time since arriving at Dunbar she felt almost light-hearted as they made their way downstairs.

The big hall was a hive of activity and already looking festive. A roaring fire had been lit in the big stone hearth, and the high mantel had been decorated with red-berried holly and trails of ivy.

Streamers had been strung across the ceiling, and swags of bright evergreens had been arranged over doorways and in every convenient corner.

A group of workmen with ladders had just finished putting up glittering gold streamers and spruce branches interspersed with waterfalls of tiny blinking lights that looked like falling snowflakes. In one corner stood a tall Christmas tree, as yet without ornament.

As Ross and Cathy reached the bottom of the stairs, one of the men came over and, with a respectful nod, said, 'Morning, Mr Dalgowan.'

'Morning, Will. It seems to be going well.'

'Aye, that it is, sir. Apart from the one or two things you asked us to leave, we've just about finished in here.'

'In that case we'll take over, and you can get on with the supper room.'

'We'll do that, right enough. It'll be all ready for the catering side to move in by mid-afternoon.'

'Right, thanks, Will. You'll be coming tonight?'

'Aye, that we will, sir. It's a bonny sight, and the missus wouldn't miss it for anything.'

With another smiling nod, he went back to his men, and a moment later they began to move their ladders and tools into the adjoining room.

Turning to Cathy, Ross asked, 'About ready to make a start?'

'Yes.' There was eagerness in her voice.

In the corner, over by the tree, was a long trestle table piled high with bunches of mistletoe waiting to be hung up, and three large cardboard boxes tied up with string.

'Tree decorations,' he told her, as he untied the boxes and lifted the lids. 'They're stored in one of the attics and brought down every Christmas. But shall we hang the mistletoe first?'

Between them they decided where the various bunches should go, and Ross used a stepladder that was standing by, to hang them.

They were about to start unpacking the boxes when Cathy brushed a strand of loose hair away from her cheek, inadvertently drawing Ross's attention to the wedding ring on her slim finger.

'Better let me take care of that,' he said. 'You don't want to lose it again.'

Before she could protest, he had slipped it off and dropped it into his pocket.

Finding a loose rubber band in the top of the first box, Cathy fastened her troublesome hair into a ponytail. Then between them they unpacked gleaming baubles of every shape and size, long glass icicles and sparkling snowflakes, sledges and lanterns, glittering tinsel and strings of fairy lights, all the precious paraphernalia of childhood Christmases long gone.

For the very top of the tree there was a choice of a magnificent silver star or a fat fairy with gauzy wings, a magic wand and a simpering expression.

For the next hour or so they worked as a team, laughing and talking like old friends, while they decorated the lower branches.

When they reached the higher ones, Cathy selected what should go where, and Ross mounted the stepladder to do her bidding.

The time flew by, and it was almost one-thirty before Ross called a halt and rang for a tray of coffee and sandwiches.

While Cathy washed her hands in one of the cloakrooms just off the hall, Ross pulled an old settle nearer to the hearth. Then, when he, too, had washed his hands, they ate picnic-fashion in front of the fire.

As she ate she thought longingly, If only this warmth and friendliness, this pleasure in being together—that he, too, seemed to feel—could go on.

Then, perhaps, when she was finally able to admit the truth, Ross might realize that she really hadn't done anything wrong that night at Ilithgow. She wasn't married, and she hadn't deliberately set out to deceive him.

Once he believed that, perhaps, against every expectation, the magic they had found together that first night *might* be rekindled.

Suddenly, along with all the troubles that had been released to beset their relationship—as though Pandora's box had been opened for a second time—was the shining gift of hope.

It might be the triumph of hope over reason, but once there it refused to be dismissed.

Lunch over, they resumed their task, and the tree started to look as festive as a Christmas tree should, while the boxes gradually emptied.

When only the very top remained to be decorated, surveying the star and the fairy, Ross said, 'Now, then, as a woman of discerning taste, which shall it be? Do you want a moment to think about it?'

'I don't need to think about it. I already know.'

'Oh?' He cocked an eyebrow at her.

'The fairy,' she said.

He groaned. 'When it was Marley's turn to choose she always picked the fairy. I never knew what it was that gave the repulsive thing such appeal.'

Cathy giggled. 'I just love her expression.'

As Ross examined the fairy's smirk, on a mischievous impulse she suggested, 'Or perhaps you could use them both?'

She saw his lips twitch. 'I see what you mean.'

He wired the star into place and arranged the fairy so that she appeared to be peering coyly around it. 'What do you think?' he asked gravely.

It looked quite ridiculous, and Cathy, who was laughing helplessly, said, 'I suggest you come down and see for yourself.'

He descended the stepladder and came to stand by her side. 'Perfect,' he approved softly. But he was looking at her laughing face rather than the tree. 'You should laugh more often.'

He was suddenly much too close for comfort, and she had taken one step backwards when he threw an imprisoning arm around her and, tall, triumphant, slightly mocking, glanced upwards.

Too late she realized that she was standing directly beneath a bunch of mistletoe.

He used his free hand to cup her chin and lift her face to his. Then his mouth was covering hers.

Instantly she was swamped, drowning in the delight of his kiss, helpless in the flood of emotion his touch had released.

He held her with an easy, complete mastery, his kiss deepening, his mouth moving against hers until she was lost, her mind unable to hold on to any coherent thought.

When he finally lifted his head and smiled down into her dazed eyes, his own eyes were cloudy with an emotion that held traces of something that could have been a wry tenderness.

He seemed about to say something of importance, when a woman's husky voice drawled, 'Well, well, well... Making use of the mistletoe already, I see.'

Just for an instant Ross looked put out, then his arms dropped away and his expression cleared as he turned to face a tall, slim woman with dark hair.

The newcomer was elegantly dressed in a silver-grey suede coat with a Cossack hat and knee-length boots.

'You look surprised to see me,' she said.

'I am, a little.'

'I don't know *why*. I told Margaret I'd probably see you all when I came to visit Daddy.'

Turning to Cathy, Ross drew her forward. 'Lena, I'd like you to meet Cathy Richardson... Cathy, may I introduce Lena Dultie, my ex-fiancée?'

Lena was one of the most beautiful women Cathy had ever seen. Her smooth black hair had the sheen of a raven's wing and her face was a perfect oval, the features clear-cut and regular. Her long-lashed eyes were so deep a blue as to look almost violet.

She was exquisitely made up and she wore diamond earrings that sparkled in the lights.

Cathy wished fervently that she had done her hair and put on some make-up. With a shiny face and a straggly ponytail,

she felt like a scruffy schoolgirl beside this elegant, sophisticated woman.

Gathering herself, she murmured, 'How do you do?'

Lena gave her a searching glance as she replied briefly and
without noticeable enthusiasm, 'It's nice to meet you.'

Obviously wondering who she was and why she was here, the
other woman went on, 'I suppose you're a guest at Beinn Mor?'

Cathy shook her head. 'I work here.'

With a little frown, Lena said a dismissive, 'Oh.'

Then, turning to Ross, she pursued, 'I hope my arrival isn't
inconvenient?'

'Of course not,' he said politely. 'It's just a little unexpected…'

With a quiet, 'Excuse me,' Cathy was about to slip away,
when Ross put a detaining hand on her arm.

'Don't go.' His glance returning to Lena, he went on, 'I
presumed you'd want to be back in London for Christmas.'

'Because Daddy's not very well, I decided to stay up here
for a while. But it's like a morgue over at Glendolan, so I
thought I'd join you for tonight's ball and perhaps stay a few
days… If that's all right by you.'

Despite the rider, she looked confident of being made welcome.

While Cathy stood quietly, Ross's light hold had relaxed, but
when, feeling *de trop*, she made a further attempt to leave, his
grip tightened once more.

His eyes on Lena, he said, 'I take it Philip's not with you?'

'No.'

'Surely he's not happy to be abandoned at the festive season?'

'As a matter of fact we're not together any longer.'

'The wedding's off?'

'Yes.'

'His decision or yours?'

'How ungallant of you! Mine, of course.'

'May I ask why?'

She sighed. 'I found I was missing you. Thinking of how it used to be.'

His voice dry, he said, 'Surely the bright lights and all the excitement of London made up for any touch of nostalgia?'

She shook her head. 'In any case there was very little in the way of excitement. When Philip came home from one of his interminable board meetings, he never wanted to go anywhere, and he was terribly jealous if I went out alone.

'Finally I realized it would be a mistake to marry a man so much older than myself, and I decided to leave him.'

'Where are you living now?'

'At the moment I'm staying with a friend until I can find somewhere suitable.'

'But obviously you'll want to remain in London.'

With a seductive glance from beneath her long black lashes, she said, 'No, not necessarily.'

He raised an eyebrow. 'Oh?'

A little uncertainly she went on, 'I've been thinking… Scotland might not be such a bad place to live, after all, so long as I could visit London every now and then.'

'Quite a change of heart,' he commented evenly.

'I hoped you'd be pleased.'

'I'm sure your father will be.'

Apparently unsure just what to make of that, she hesitated before going on, 'By the way, as I passed Beinn Mor I stopped to have a quick word with Janet. She mentioned that you have no *personal* guest staying with you…'

At that moment the housekeeper appeared.

Turning to her, Ross asked, 'You wanted to speak to me, Mrs Fife?'

'It was about Miss Dultie, Mr Ross. Dougal has brought her

luggage in, but there's no room ready because I didn't know she was expected.'

'That's quite all right, Mrs Fife, no one knew,' Ross said smoothly. 'Miss Dultie intended her visit to be a surprise…'

The housekeeper's expression showed exactly what she thought of such surprises.

'So I would be grateful if you could make up a room for her.'

'Of course, Mr Ross.'

This obviously wasn't at all what Lena had been hoping for, and she said quickly, 'But, Ross, as you have no personal guest, and you'll be on your own, I thought I might stay in your suite…provide a bit of company…'

'That's very kind of you, Lena,' he said silkily. 'But I wasn't planning to be on my own.'

As the other woman frowned, and Cathy wondered exactly what he had meant by that remark, he nodded to Mrs Fife, who turned and hurried away.

'Now, shall we all go along to the study, and I'll ring for a pot of tea and some sandwiches?' he suggested briskly.

But Cathy, having been forced into the position of unwilling listener, had had more than enough.

Standing her ground, she looked Ross in the eye and said, 'I'd like to go straight back to the flat. It's starting to get dark, so it shouldn't be long before Carl's home.'

Somewhat to her surprise, he agreed, 'Certainly, if that's what you want. Perhaps you'd care to come upstairs with me and fetch your bag?'

He turned to Lena, who seemed about to accompany them, and, his voice pleasant, suggested, 'If you'd like to go along to my study and order the tea, I'll join you there in a minute or so.'

Though it was phrased as a request, it was undoubtedly an

order, and, obviously recognizing it as such, after a fractional pause Lena agreed meekly, 'Of course, if that's what you want.'

As, a hand at Cathy's waist, Ross escorted her up the stairs, she said, as though the words were forced out of her, 'Lena's very beautiful.'

'Yes,' he agreed. 'She's one of the most beautiful women I've ever known.'

Just hearing him say that made Cathy feel hollow inside, slightly sick.

But what had she expected? she asked herself wearily. If he had chosen to deny it, having seen his ex-fiancée, she wouldn't have believed him. An ex-fiancée who had quite quickly made it plain that she would prefer to drop the 'ex' and be reinstated.

Catching her bottom lip between her teeth, Cathy bit hard. After the way Lena had left him for another man, would Ross take her back?

No doubt he'd be only too pleased to if he still felt anything for her. And, after all, the break had never really been final. Lena had never really let go...

But if he *was* tempted to take her back, why hadn't he allowed her to move straight into his suite, as she had been only too willing to do?

Perhaps he had decided to make her wait, to punish her a little first?

As soon as they reached the suite, Cathy went through to the living room to collect her bag.

The room was familiar and cosy, with its blazing log fire and standard lamps, and the rich red velvet curtains drawn against the snow-covered landscape and the cold grey dusk.

Knowing she was unlikely to be here again, she glanced around for the last time and felt a dull ache of regret. As far as

Ross was concerned she was merely another man's wife, a woman who had neither morals nor self-respect.

Now Lena was here, and more than willing to share his bed, he would no doubt forget his earlier demand that *she* should be available whenever he wanted her.

She knew she should feel pleased and relieved. But in reality she felt sad and miserably jealous. All the afternoon's new-found hope and optimism had vanished, leaving only a sense of loss, of desolation.

She was heading for the door when Ross, who had been standing quietly watching her, moved to open it. Taking a deep breath, she glanced up at him and, trying to sound cheerful, said, 'Thank you for today. Decorating the tree was fun.'

'I enjoyed it, too.'

She was moving past him when he put a detaining hand on her arm. 'You'll be at the ball tonight.'

It was a statement rather than a question, but knowing she couldn't bear to watch Lena and him together, she said, 'I've got a bit of a headache and I'd like an early night. So I may not come if Carl doesn't mind...'

'I mind,' Ross said flatly. 'I want you there.'

At that instant his phone rang. 'Wait,' he said tersely and moved to answer it.

'Ross Dalgowan... Yes... Yes... When...?'

Cathy was about to disobey his order and slip away, when the look on his face stopped her even before he held up a warning hand.

'What happened...?'

While he listened, he crossed the room in a few strides and, taking her arm, led her back to one of the armchairs by the fire.

Scared by the grimness of his expression, she went without protest and, sinking into the chair, watched his face in silence.

For what seemed an age, but could only have been a minute or so, he listened intently, before demanding, 'You're quite sure...? Yes... Yes. If the situation should change...? You will...' His taut expression relaxed. 'Right... Many thanks for letting me know.'

When he'd replaced the receiver, she asked, a shade unsteadily, 'What's wrong?'

'The group doing the winter survival course were on their way back when there was an accident...'

White to the lips, she whispered, 'Carl...?'

'I gather that two men were slightly injured, and Carl was one of them. But he's quite safe and in no danger,' Ross added firmly.

'Thank God,' she said huskily, and, suddenly starting to tremble, she covered her face with shaking hands.

After her parents had died, Carl had been at once her responsibility and her reason for living. Always an outdoor man, an experienced climber and a natural on skis, it had been his dream to do what he was doing now, and she had struggled hard to help him realize that dream.

This was his first post, and just for a moment, on hearing about the accident, she had visualized it all ending in tragedy.

The relief of knowing he was safe had been overwhelming, and she had to fight to get a grip on her emotions.

When she'd succeeded, she lowered her hands and, taking a deep breath, said, 'I'm sorry.'

'There's nothing to be sorry for,' Ross told her gently. 'A lot of woman wouldn't have been nearly so self-controlled.'

Some colour started to creep back into her cheeks, and she asked, 'What happened, exactly?'

'I don't know the ins and outs of it—all I know is that the whole party are on their way to Glendesh and it may be tomorrow morning before they're able to get transport back home. My informant assured me that some time this evening Kevin will be calling to give me more details and, in the meantime, if there's any change in the situation he'll be sure to let me know.'

As he finished speaking, the door opened and Lena appeared. She had discarded her coat and looked stunning in a clinging blue dress that made the most of her slender figure.

Looking anything but happy, she complained, 'Really, Ross, I don't know what's happened to your manners! You never used to treat your guests in such a cavalier fashion. The tea I ordered arrived ages ago and it's gone cold while I've been sitting waiting for you...'

Going over to her, he took her hand. 'I do beg your pardon.' He sounded genuinely regretful. 'But I had an urgent phone call. Kevin, along with our newest member of staff and a party of guests, were on their way back to Beinn Mor when they met with an accident. Why don't you come and sit down? I'll ask for another tray of tea, and while we have it I'll tell you as much as I know.'

Looking somewhat mollified, Lena allowed herself to be led over to the fire and seated.

Seizing her chance, Cathy grabbed her bag and was heading for the door when Ross asked politely, 'Won't you stay for some tea?'

Though her throat was dry, and she felt parched, she said a firm, 'No, thank you.'

'Certain? After all, there's nothing to rush back for now.'

Turning a deaf ear, she kept walking.

Ross reached the door first and opened it. But, as he had done previously, he held it so she couldn't go through it until he allowed her to.

'Sure you're feeling all right?'

'Quite sure,' she told him.

'No worries?'

She shook her head. 'None.'

'Then I'll expect to see you at the ball tonight.'

But knowing that Carl wouldn't be there, and that Lena most certainly *would*, she had absolutely no intention of going.

She was preparing to turn away when Ross took her chin between the thumb and fingers of his free hand and lifted her face to his.

'Don't think for an instant that I don't know precisely what you have in mind,' he said quietly.

'I've no idea what you mean.' She tried to sound innocent and failed miserably.

His grey eyes looking deeply into hers, he said with soft menace, 'You know perfectly well what I mean. But if you like I'll spell it out for you. Don't imagine you can get away with hiding in the flat and not coming.'

'I don't understand why you want me to come when you have your ex-fiancée,' she protested helplessly.

'Perhaps I prefer a threesome.'

Gritting her teeth, she said, 'Well, *I* don't.'

'Too bad. I want you there by eight o'clock at the very latest.'

'I haven't anything to wear,' she said in desperation. 'The only party dress I have was the one I was wearing the night I set off to walk back from Beinn Mor...'

'The dress you wore to dinner the first night you were here will do fine.'

'Oh, but I—'

'No more excuses,' he said brusquely. 'You'd better be there, unless you want me to come and fetch you.'

She could easily believe that he meant it, and her soft mouth tightened.

He smiled a little crookedly, then, bending his fair head, he kissed her slowly and deliberately on the mouth—a kiss that left no doubt that they were lovers—before stepping back.

She knew Lena was watching, and she strongly suspected that Ross had kissed her purposely to annoy his ex-fiancée.

Her heart racing, and angry that he had used her to make the other woman jealous, she fled along the corridor, down the stairs and to the flat.

Fumbling for the keys, she let herself in and went through to the kitchen to make herself a cup of tea.

No matter what Ross said, she had no intention of going to the ball, she told herself firmly, and if he *did* come to fetch her she wouldn't open the door.

But then she wouldn't need to. He had a key. And as there were no bolts on the doors, if he *wanted* to walk straight in she couldn't prevent him.

So where did that leave her?

At his mercy.

By seven-thirty she had showered and dressed, taken her hair up into a gleaming chignon and put on some make-up. Just in case.

Only too aware that her costume jewellery would look cheap and tawdry against Lena's diamonds, she left her ears and throat bare.

Ross still had the wedding ring he had slipped into his pocket earlier, so her only adornment was the small oval watch she wore on a plain black strap.

Though something had impelled her to get ready, as the hands of the clock moved closer to eight, she was still determined not to go.

But if she didn't, would Ross really come to fetch her as he'd threatened?

Now he had Lena, it was on the cards that he wouldn't. And he certainly wouldn't if Lena had any say in the matter.

Cathy sighed. Though normally she was composed and even-tempered, tonight she was in a strange mood. Missing Carl's reassuring presence, she felt tired and depressed, but at the same time on edge and restless, unsure what to do with herself.

If she went to the ball she would be on her own, and the thought of having to watch Lena and Ross together was almost unbearable.

No, she wouldn't go. *Couldn't* go. She would take herself off to bed with a book...

Deep in thought, she jumped when the clock on the mantelpiece struck eight. Almost at the same moment there was a knock at the outer door.

She knew instinctively that it wasn't Ross. He would never have knocked in that irresolute manner.

Frowning a little, she went to see who the unexpected caller was.

When she opened the door, it was to find Robert standing there, looking unsure of himself and of his welcome. He was wearing evening dress and a black bow tie that was slightly crooked. His faced glowed as though freshly scrubbed, and his receding hair was brushed back neatly.

She smiled at him. 'Well, hello.'

'I hope you don't mind me barging in like this, but I heard about the accident and the fact that the whole party's been delayed, and I came to say how pleased I was that Carl and everyone are safe.'

'Thank you, that's very nice of you.'

After a slight hesitation, he went on, 'Ross mentioned that you would still be coming to the ball...'

Cathy was about to say she'd decided not to when Robert

added tentatively, 'And I wondered…as you're on your own…if you'd like an escort?'

Guessing he'd had to psyche himself up to ask, and unwilling to disappoint him, she found herself saying, 'Thank you, I'd love one. I didn't fancy going alone.'

He looked so happy and relieved that she couldn't regret her impulse.

Smiling at him, she picked up her evening bag and closed the door behind her.

Once outside, she could hear music and the sound of revelry and laughter.

Knowing she needed to make an effort, if only for Robert's sake, she slipped her hand through his arm and said brightly, 'Now I know there's no need to worry about Carl, let's go and have some fun.'

He smiled at her. 'Let's.'

When they reached the main hall it was a scene of festive gaiety. The massive logs in the fireplace were blazing, the chandeliers were lit, and all the lights were twinkling like softly falling snowflakes.

Since she had last seen it, a well-stocked portable bar had been set up at one end, and waiters were circulating with trays of champagne.

Chairs and small tables had been placed in groups around the perimeter of the hall, and, finding an empty one, Robert pulled out a chair for her.

A sizeable band had taken over the minstrels' gallery and was playing a lively quickstep, to which quite a number of couples were circling the floor.

Amongst the throng of dancers, Cathy caught sight of Lena and Ross, and her heart seemed to turn over in her breast.

They made an outstandingly handsome couple, Ross in an

immaculate dinner jacket and black tie, and Lena wearing a daring dress with no back and very little front. It was the colour of flame, with elaborate silver embroidery that ran from the bust line to where the skirt was split up to the thigh.

She looked a million dollars, her mouth and nails as vivid as the dress, and the diamonds at her throat and ears sparkling under the lights.

His blond head bent towards her gleaming black one, their steps matching perfectly, they were dancing as if they were made for each other.

Seeing them like that made Cathy feel a kind of numb despair.

Noticing the shadow that had passed across her face, Robert asked anxiously, 'Anything wrong?'

'No, no, nothing's wrong,' she assured him and forced a smile. 'I was just thinking… Carl was really looking forward to the ball. It's a shame he and the others have had to miss it.'

Then, wondering if her words might have deflated her companion, she added quickly, 'I'm very lucky that you were free to escort me.'

The tips of his ears going pink, he mumbled, 'It's my pleasure.' Then with his usual diffidence he asked, 'Would you like a glass of champagne? Or perhaps there's something you'd sooner have?'

'Champagne will be lovely, thank you.'

Signalling a waiter, he helped himself to two glasses and handed one to Cathy.

'Thank you.'

The band was playing a tango, and, guessing that Robert would sooner stay where he was, she mentioned how much she liked Scotland, or at least what she'd seen of it, and asked him whereabouts he'd been born and brought up.

Given an interested listener, he talked happily while they sat and sipped their champagne.

Though to all intents and purposes she gave Robert her full attention, Cathy's eyes were frequently drawn to the dance floor as she found herself searching for a certain fair head. But for a while now she had seen no sign of Ross or his beautiful partner.

She had taken only a sip or two from her second glass of champagne when Ross appeared by her side.

Removing the glass from her nerveless fingers, he put it down on the table beside her bag and said to Robert, 'If I may, I'd like to borrow Cathy for a minute or so?'

Though he looked a little surprised, Robert agreed accommodatingly, 'Of course.'

Ross's hand closed around her elbow, and before she could catch her breath she found herself being urged to her feet.

At that instant Lena hurried up and, putting a possessive, red-tipped hand on Ross's arm, said, 'When I came back from powdering my nose you'd vanished. Where on earth did you disappear to?'

'I was in my study taking a phone call. Now, if you'll excuse us,' he said firmly. 'I'm sure Robert will take care of you for a little while.'

Robert, who had risen to his feet, said with an attempt at polite gallantry that almost hid his lack of enthusiasm, 'I'll be pleased to.' Pulling out a chair for Lena, he added, 'Would you like a glass of champagne?'

Clearly ruffled, she told him shortly, 'I never drink alcohol. It's bad for my complexion.'

Robert's prominent Adam's apple moved up and down as he swallowed uncomfortably. 'Then, a soft drink of some kind?'

Before she heard the answer, Cathy found herself hurried in the direction of Ross's study, still carrying in her mind's eye a picture of Lena's angry, suspicious face.

CHAPTER TEN

As THE study door closed behind them, fearing there might have been some bad news, Cathy asked anxiously, 'You've heard from Kevin?'

'Yes, a little while ago. I now know more or less what happened.'

Taking her elbow, he led her to the fire and settled her into an armchair before dropping into a chair opposite.

Her eyes on his face, she waited.

Impressed by her quiet self-control, he began without preamble. 'The group were making a steep descent on Scoran when one of the men in the party lost his footing and fell into a deep fissure.

'When they failed to get any response to their shouts, Carl went down after him with a rope and a lightweight harness... I've no idea why Carl went rather than Kevin...'

'Though skiing has always been his first love, Carl is an experienced mountaineer,' Cathy said. 'His father started to take him climbing almost as soon as he could walk. By the time he was fifteen, after tackling various orientation, winter survival and mountain rescue courses, he was as skilled as many a man twice his age.' Then, realizing what she'd said, she added hastily, 'Or so he once told me.'

'I see. That explains it. Well, the man who fell had been knocked unconscious, so Carl fitted the harness and the rope, and they got ready to pull him up. But because loose, jagged rocks beneath the snow and ice made it particularly dangerous, Carl climbed with him.

'They were almost at the top when a large chunk of snow and ice broke off and fell, taking some of the rocks with it. Carl succeeded in shielding the injured man but was himself struck on the shoulder, and one arm was put out of action.

'Somehow he managed to hold on to the rope, and after a struggle they were both pulled to safety. Kevin had already been in touch with the Mountain Rescue Service, and, to cut a long story short, both the injured men were picked up by air ambulance and flown to the Glendesh Hospital.

'The rest of the party, some of whom were badly shaken, made it to the nearest road, where rescue vehicles were waiting to take them into Glendesh.

'The latest report from the hospital is that both men are comfortable. Carl has a dislocated shoulder, while the man he saved seems to have escaped with cuts and bruises.

'Just as a precaution they're both being kept in overnight for observation, while the rest have been put up at the Glendesh Hotel. But the whole party confidently expect to be driven back to Dunbar in time for Christmas lunch.'

Cathy sent up a silent prayer of thanks.

In the wide grate a log settled, sending a shower of bright sparks up the chimney.

Watching her face in the flickering firelight, the winged brows, the lovely curve of her mouth, the shadow of her long lashes on her cheeks, Ross sighed.

In spite, or perhaps because, of all the unheavals she had had to face, she had a quality of stillness, an inner strength, a kind of serenity that found an answering echo in himself.

Seeing her and Lena together had dispersed any faint doubts that might have lingered at the back of his mind. Now he knew exactly where he was going and what was right for him.

In the warmth from the fire her eyelids had started to droop, and he guessed that in another minute or so she would be fast asleep.

He wanted to stay here with her in this quiet room, but there were people waiting for them and, as host, he had certain duties to perform.

Reluctantly he said, 'Well, I suppose we'd better be moving.' As she blinked, he added, 'Your escort will be getting worried.'

Something about the gleam in his eye made her accuse, '*You* sent Robert to fetch me.'

'Not at all. I merely happened to mention that, with Carl being away, you wouldn't have an escort. I knew you'd come like a lamb with Robert, so it seemed the easiest way to do it.'

'You devious swine,' she muttered.

He clicked his tongue in reproof. 'That's no way for a nicely brought up young lady to talk.' Then, before she could retaliate he said, 'Now, let's go, otherwise Lena will have reduced poor Robert to a nervous wreck.'

As they neared the table they saw the two were sitting in silence. Lena appeared to be bored stiff, while Robert wore a hunted look.

He rose to his feet at Cathy's approach, his expression changing to one of relief.

Lena rose, too, and, her voice plaintive, said to Ross, 'Just listen to what the band's playing. I was starting to think you were going to let me miss my favourite number.'

Looking down at her, he said, 'My dear Lena, I can't believe a woman as beautiful as you wouldn't have a choice of partners.'

'But, darling,' she purred, 'it wouldn't be the same with anyone else.'

'In that case—' Ross turned to the other two '—if you'll excuse us?'

Sinking onto her chair, Cathy was wondering how soon she could escape without hurting Robert's feelings, when Ross caught her eye and held it.

A warning note in his voice, he said, 'I'll be back in a while to claim a dance, and after that perhaps we can all go into supper together.'

Cathy was horrified, and, judging by the silence that followed his proposal, neither of the others were enamoured of the idea either.

Lena was the only one to voice a protest. 'But, Ross, wouldn't it be nicer to—'

He gave her a cool glance that effectively stopped the little rush of words.

With a shrug of her bare shoulders, she gave in and allowed herself to be led onto the floor.

When Lena and Ross began to move to a rhumba rhythm, Robert turned to Cathy and, clearing his throat, asked, 'Would you like to dance?'

He sounded anything but eager, and aware that he was scared of doing Latin American she said, 'Thank you, but I'd just as soon sit and watch for a while.' Smiling his relief, he relaxed.

She told him about the phone call and, when that topic of conversation had been exhausted, asked him about his job.

It was immediately apparent that he enjoyed what he did and that he was more than willing to talk about the running of the estate.

He had just finished telling her about the new herd of deer they were introducing, when Margaret and Janet appeared from the throng.

'So, there you are,' Margaret said cheerfully. 'I'm so glad you decided to come. Ross said he'd try and persuade you. After all, what's the point of sitting on your own?

'It's a pity that Carl and the others couldn't be here, but it's such a relief to know they're all safe and relatively unharmed. When I talked to Kevin on the phone earlier, he said your husband's a real hero, and if it hadn't been for his skill and courage, the accident might have had a much more serious outcome.'

'As it is,' Janet chimed in, 'they'll all be home safe tomorrow, thank the Lord. It's lovely having Christmas lunch at Dunbar…'

Margaret agreed, adding, 'But it would have been a great deal more enjoyable if Lena hadn't turned up. Her visits always unsettle Ross. I don't think he ever properly got over her. I don't know why she keeps coming… It's as if the dratted woman can't bear to let go—' Then, looking flustered, she said, 'I'm sorry. I really shouldn't have spoken so frankly…'

'Why shouldn't you?' Janet said stoutly. 'After all, it's what everyone's thinking. By the way, when I was talking to her earlier, I noticed she wasn't wearing her engagement ring. And she asked pointedly if Ross had a *personal* guest for Christmas. I think she's all set to get her hooks into him again. I hope to goodness he has more sense than to take her back…'

Catching Margaret's warning glance, she said defiantly, 'Well, it's not as if anyone likes her. *You* don't like her, do you, Rob?'

Obviously disconcerted at being put on the spot, Robert stammered, 'I…I don't really know her all that well.'

'Go on, be honest.'

'Well, no… To tell you the truth, I don't.'

To save him any further embarrassment Margaret changed the subject, and they discussed the ball and how well it was all going.

Pressed to sit down, Margaret and Janet refused, on the grounds that they would need to circulate, and drifted away.

When the Latin American session ended and the band began to play an old Gershwin tune, with a smile of relief, Robert led Cathy onto the floor.

But while her feet moved in time to the music, her mind was obsessed with thoughts of Ross and Lena and a growing certainty that he *would* take her back.

Some half an hour later they were still dancing when she caught sight of Ross and his sister returning from the direction of the study. As she watched, Margaret stood on tiptoe to kiss his cheek, before she walked away, smiling.

The last number before supper was announced, and at the same instant Ross appeared at Cathy's side and said smoothly, 'My dance, I think.'

Robert relinquished his partner, and Ross took Cathy in his arms.

It was a slow foxtrot, dreamy and romantic. But, remembering how Lena had melted against him, and wondering why he'd insisted on having this dance, she held herself stiffly, keeping several inches of space between their two bodies.

Ross bent his head and, his lips brushing her cheek, murmured softly, 'Anyone might think you hated having to dance with me.'

'Anyone might be right,' she said rebelliously.

He paid her back for that remark by nipping the edge of her ear between his teeth.

She gave a little indignant gasp.

'Perhaps you'd prefer me to kiss you?'

When she said nothing, his lips traced the pure curve of her cheek and jaw and began to wander down the side of her neck.

Shuddering, she whispered hoarsely, 'Please, don't do that.'

'I'll stop when you relax and try to look as if you enjoy dancing with me.'

She said, 'I'll try, but it won't be easy,' and heard his soft laugh.

However, the mood of the music was beginning to weave its magic and when, almost unconsciously, she started to relax, his arm tightened around her, drawing her closer.

It would probably be the last time they would ever dance together, she realized, the last time she would feel his arms around her, so if that was the case, she might as well try to enjoy it.

By the time the band moved on to another romantic tune, a poignant melody with the shiver of strings, her eyes were closed, her head was on his shoulder and his cheek was against her hair.

The music ended, and Cathy came out of her dream to find herself face to face with Lena. The other woman's expression held such jealous rage that she almost flinched.

But that look was instantly gone as, turning to smile at Ross, Lena asked gaily, 'Supper now?'

She had been dancing with a good-looking young man who, clearly bedazzled by his partner, seemed about to accompany them. But she shook him off with such an icy glare that Cathy felt sorry for him.

As they moved towards the supper room Lena stopped at one of the tables to pick up a triangular stole with silver embroidery that matched her dress.

As Ross put the beautiful thing around her shoulders, she said, 'Thank you, darling,' and, tilting her head sideways, offered her gleaming red lips for his kiss.

But he didn't appear to notice, and when Robert came up to join them and handed Cathy her bag, the moment had passed.

The large supper room was very nicely decorated, and a substantial buffet had been laid out along the length of one wall.

Cathy had never felt less like eating, but together with everyone else she helped herself to a plate of food before they sat down at one of the tables.

Though Ross, effortlessly assuming the role of host, put Lena's stole carefully over the back of her chair, poured wine for them all and talked lightly and easily, the little gathering was a strained one.

Cathy could find nothing to say, and Lena, obviously put out by Ross's refusal to kiss her, seemed to be brooding, so it was the two men who carried the conversation.

A selection of delectable sweets was brought around on trolleys, followed, after a decent interval, by coffee and liqueurs.

Cups, cream, sugar and a pot of coffee had just been placed on their table by one of the waiters, when Robert turned to Cathy and began, 'I understand that Carl—'

A split second later Cathy cried out with shock as the pot full of hot black liquid overturned and went cascading down her.

She sprang to her feet, aware only of the searing pain as the clinging material of her dress held the scalding coffee against her skin.

Urgent hands caught hold of her, and in what seemed to be one deft movement, Ross had pulled down the zip, stripped the dress from her, and wrapped Lena's stole round her, sarong-wise.

A second later, before most people had realized anything was amiss, he was hurrying her out of the supper room, across the hall and up the stairs.

Trying to struggle free, she protested, 'I want to go back to the flat... I don't want to—'

'We're doing this my way.'

As soon as they reached his suite he hustled her through to the bathroom, pulled off her sandals, twitched away the stole, and thrust her, still clad in her coffee-stained bra and briefs, unceremoniously into the shower.

She gasped as the cold water sprayed over her heated skin and would have instinctively stepped back, but he said almost savagely, 'Stay where you are until I tell you.'

Suddenly seeing the ridiculous side, she observed, 'This is getting to be a habit.'

He pulled off his jacket, rolled up his shirtsleeves and, reaching for the first-aid box, advised, 'Save the funny cracks until we know if there's been any harm done.'

After perhaps half a minute, the burning pain caused by the scalding coffee had eased, and she began to shiver uncontrollably.

'Are you all right?' he asked.

Through chattering teeth she said, 'Oh, f-f-fine.' The sarcasm failed utterly.

He turned off the water and, having helped her out, started to remove her sodden undies, but she pushed his hands away.

'Don't be a fool,' he said impatiently. 'I've no intention of molesting you. I just want you dry so I can spray some of this on.'

'This' proved to be a canister of fresh-smelling analgesic, which soothed what few red marks remained, before she found herself wrapped in a soft bathrobe.

Her wet hair was escaping from its chignon, so he took out the remaining pins and, picking up a brush, turned on the blow-drier.

When the silken mass was almost dry, he led her to a chair in front of the living-room fire and gently pushed her into it.

The first adrenaline rush over, and reminded of the fact that she was once again trapped in his suite without clothes, she bit her lip.

'How are you feeling now?' he asked. 'There's at least one doctor present if you—'

'No, no… There's absolutely no need.'

'Sure?'

'Yes, quite sure.' Knowing that, in spite of everything, she owed him a debt of gratitude, she added a shade stiltedly, 'Thanks to your quick action, I won't have so much as a blister.'

'You don't sound particularly grateful.' His tone held dark mockery.

'Well, I am. I just don't think there was any need for you to turn into Atilla the Hun.'

With a grin he told her, 'Baby, you ain't seen nothin' yet.'

He disappeared from view for a moment or two and returned carrying Lena's stole, his jacket and a glass containing a milky-looking liquid.

Handing her the glass, he said, 'Drink this.'

'What is it?' Suspicion edged her tone.

'It's a painkiller, just in case.'

He rolled down his shirtsleeves and pulled on his jacket, before adding briskly, 'Wait here. There's something I have to deal with.'

As he headed for the door, she asked uncertainly, 'Where are you going?'

'To let Robert know you're all right and return Lena's stole.'

'Oh… But surely you intend to rejoin her? Go back to the party…?'

'I don't intend to do anything of the kind,' he said decidedly. 'I'll only be a short time, so stay exactly where you are until I get back.'

Watching the door close behind him, Cathy found herself wondering why he'd played things the way he had. Why he'd insisted on bringing her to his suite when later, no doubt, Lena would be joining him here.

She stiffened as a sudden, most unpleasant thought struck

her: suppose the other woman insisted on coming back with him *now*?

Agitation made her heart start to race. What was she to do? She couldn't just sit here. But neither could she go down the main stairs and across the hall wearing a loose bathrobe miles too big for her.

Surely there must be some way, a servants' staircase, that she could use to get back to the flat without being seen?

But if there was she didn't know it, and in any case her keys were in her evening bag, which had been left in the supper room…

A moment or two later, Ross returned.

To her very great relief he was alone.

Looking grimly satisfied, he discarded his jacket and bow tie before dropping into the chair opposite.

Anxious to get away, she said, 'If you would be kind enough to show me the back stairs…I'd really like to go now.'

'Go? Go where?'

'To the flat, of course,' she said shortly.

'I thought, as Carl won't be back, you might like to stay here.'

'No, I *wouldn't* like to stay here.' Without really thinking, she added bitterly, 'I've never liked the idea of three in a bed.'

'Pity,' he drawled, leaning back in his chair and stretching his long legs indolently. 'I have a feeling it could be fun.'

Her cheeks flaming, she jumped to her feet and said in a strangled voice, 'I'd like to go.'

'And I'd like you to stay. But before you make up your mind, I want you to try something on.'

He stepped behind her, and, before she could gather her wits, a cool weight had settled around her slender throat.

Then, his hands on her upper arms, he turned her slightly so that she could see both their reflections in a gilt-framed oval mirror that hung above an occasional table.

He was a good head taller than she was, and the lamplight brought his handsome features into prominence, made his grey eyes gleam and turned his blond hair, hair that always looked as if it wanted to curl, to pale gold.

She stared at him, unable to look away, and their gazes meshed.

Until, as though he'd willed it, her eyes dropped to a beautiful necklace that, sparkling and glittering in its delicate antique setting, fell in an exquisite rain of diamonds between the wide lapels of the robe.

Staring at it, she felt her jaw drop.

Reaching round, he put a finger beneath her chin and observed gently, 'Your mouth's open.'

Then, taking her hand, he put a pair of long drop earrings into her palm. 'These are the earrings that complete the set, but it might be better if you fix them yourself.'

Like someone in a trance, she fastened them to her small lobes while he watched her in the mirror.

The vision that looked back at her took her breath away. As she stared at this stranger, Ross asked, 'What do you think of them?'

'I've never seen anything so lovely,' she breathed.

He smiled. 'I'm pleased you like them.'

'Any woman would like them, they're…' Suddenly realizing *why* he'd got her to try them on, she stopped abruptly.

An angry flush rising in her cheeks, she reached to remove them, but he caught her hands and prevented her. 'Don't take them off. I want you to wear them while I make love to you.'

'I've no intention of letting you make love to me, and I *hate* the idea of wearing jewels obviously intended for another woman.'

'But they're not intended for another woman. They're for you.'

He sounded as if he meant it, and, totally bewildered, she said, 'Is this some kind of joke?'

'No, it isn't a joke.'

'But you can't give me these.'

'I already have.'

'I can't possibly accept them. Even if they're not real diamonds, they must be worth a considerable amount because of the beautiful workmanship...'

'The diamonds are real enough. My great-grandfather gave them to my great-grandmother, and since then they've been handed down to the eldest son's bride. My mother always loved them, but when she left she felt she had no right to take them.'

Seeing he wasn't joking, Cathy burst out, 'I don't understand. How can you possibly give them to *me*? You've just said they should go to your bride when you marry.'

'Well, I know it's a little premature, as I haven't actually asked you yet, but I was rather hoping we could be married quite soon.'

As she gaped at him, he smiled and said, 'My love, did you really believe I would have deliberately seduced another man's wife?'

'You *knew*?'

'Yes, but not immediately. At first I was angry, shattered, bitterly disillusioned. You'd come into my arms so innocently, so shyly, yet with a warmth and passion that sent me up in flames. To realize that it had all been a sham reinforced my doubts as to whether any female could really be trusted... It was like a blow in the face to think that the woman I'd fallen in love with at first sight, and who had seemed to feel the same way about me, was just a cheating little bitch.

'But there was something about you, a quality of goodness, of honesty, that made that assumption ring untrue, that made me wonder. And right from the start a couple of things didn't add up. The hesitant answers you gave when I questioned you, and Carl's attitude. Though he was clearly very fond of you, he didn't have the look either of a new husband or an established lover, and I needed to know if you were sleeping together—'

Though she hadn't really been taking in much since those wonderful words, *I was rather hoping we could be married quite soon*, she glanced up at that.

Noting her expression, he broke off and, smiling wryly, admitted, 'Yes, I went into your flat, and when I found you were using separate rooms I hired a private investigator in London to check things out.

'The morning after your attempt to walk back from Beinn Mor, I was waiting for you in the study. I knew Carl had left early, and when you didn't show up by nine-thirty I began to get concerned. I went along to the flat and let myself in. You were still sleeping peacefully, with Onions beside you, and Carl had left a very enlightening note...'

'Of course,' she breathed. 'He called me Sis.'

'Which told me nearly all I needed to know and made me furious.'

'So that's why you were so horrible to me.'

'Believe me, I could have been a great deal worse. The way I felt that minute I could cheerfully have put you over my knee. That is, until relief took over. But even that relief was mingled with anger when I thought of all you'd put me through.

'Then when I gave you back the ring, which was obviously not *your* ring, I pushed you as hard as I could, determined to make you admit the truth. But I couldn't break you.

'The investigator I hired was very efficient, and first thing this morning he came up with a detailed dossier of both your life and Carl's.'

'So you know everything?'

'Pretty well everything. Including your disastrous first marriage, which you can tell me about some time, and the way Carl's wedding plans collapsed at the last minute.'

'I can't tell you how sorry I am. Neither of us wanted to have to lie and deceive people we liked. I would have apologized earlier if I'd—'

He shook his head. 'All I wanted was to hear you admit the truth. That's why I kept up the pressure. But while we were decorating the tree you were so sweet, so lovely, that I almost relented and brought everything into the open myself. The only thing that held me back was the fear that after the way I'd treated you, you might simply walk out. I was partly reassured by your reaction when I kissed you under the mistletoe, but before I could say anything, Lena turned up.

'Though I was far from pleased to see her, her unexpected visit proved to be very useful. It removed any last faint doubt about my feelings for her, and finally enabled me to cut any ties with the past. And, though you tried to hide it, your reaction convinced me that you cared for me enough to forgive the way I'd treated you and agree to marry me.'

Though Cathy had never been happier, one anxiety remained. 'I don't know what your sister will think when she knows.'

'Earlier this evening I talked to Marley and told her everything. Believe me, she understands... And, incidentally, she gave us her blessing.

'Now, there are two things I still need to know. Firstly, how soon will you marry me?'

Her heart full to overflowing, her eyes shining, she said, 'As soon as you like,' and was rewarded with a lingering kiss.

At length, after reluctantly freeing her lips, he murmured, 'Now, as we're officially engaged, I'd like you to wear this…'

He took a small leather box from the nearby bookcase, and a moment later he had slipped a beautiful diamond solitaire onto her third finger.

As she gazed at it wordlessly, he added, 'Of course, if you don't like it, or you don't care for the idea of wearing a ring that's belonged to someone else…'

It was the loveliest ring imaginable, and a perfect fit, but still she hesitated.

'Don't worry, my love,' Ross said gently. 'I quite understand. The first chance we get we'll go and choose something different.'

As he reached for her hand to take it off again, she asked in a rush, 'Whose ring was it?'

'My mother's. Toby bought it for "the love of his life", and she always wore it. Just before she died, she gave it to me and said she hoped I'd give it to the love of my life.'

'It's the most beautiful ring I've ever seen,' Cathy said softly, 'and I'd love to wear it.'

Watching her face, the way relief and pleasure mingled, he said, 'You were afraid that it might have been Lena's…?'

Flushing a little, she said, 'I'm sorry.'

He shook his head. 'There's nothing to be sorry about. And, just to set your mind completely at rest, I never even thought of giving Lena this. Her engagement ring, which she chose herself, was a half hoop of rubies, which she kept. Now, where was I?'

'You said there were two things you needed to know…' Cathy prompted.

'Oh, yes… The second one is, are you certain you have no ill effects from the coffee incident?'

'Positive,' she said, her voice dismissive. 'I'm not even sure how it happened.'

'I am,' he said grimly. 'The waiter had put the coffee pot down close to you, and Lena decided to get rid of the opposition.'

As Cathy gaped at him, he went on, 'You'd turned to listen to what Robert was saying, but I happened to glance in her direction and I saw her knock it over. When I went down to return her stole, she made the excuse that she'd been about to pour the coffee and it was an accident. But I was certain it had been quite deliberate, and Robert, who had also seen the whole thing, was able to confirm that.

'I told her she had half an hour to pack her bags and then I would send Dougal up to carry them out to the car.

'But enough of Lena. We're wasting precious time...' As he finished speaking, the clock began to chime twelve.

'Christmas Day,' Cathy murmured as the last note died away.

'Happy Christmas, my heart's darling.' He took her in his arms and kissed her with a passionate urgency that sent her up in flames.

The living-room fire had dwindled into glowing ashes, and, switching off the lamps, he led her through to the bedroom.

There, the logs were still blazing, filling the room with the scent of pine, while the flickering firelight cast long, dancing shadows on the white walls and ceiling.

As he paused to kiss her once more, his hand slipped between the lapels of the robe to caress her breast and tease the nipple into life.

Hearing her gasp of pleasure, and feeling her heart begin to beat faster beneath his palm, he asked softly, 'About ready for bed?'

'Mmm...' she murmured, and snuggled against him.

'That's good. But first I want to give you your Christmas present.'

All her attention focused on the delightful things his fingers were doing to her, she said abstractedly, 'But you've already given me so much, and I've nothing to give you.'

'That's where you're wrong. You can give me everything I've ever wanted, everything I've ever dreamt about and hoped for. But first of all see what you think of yours.'

He reached for a small square package wrapped in gold paper that stood on the bureau.

It was quite heavy, and, sinking down in the nearest chair, she set it down on her lap. Then, stripping off the gold foil, she opened the blue velvet-covered lid and lifted out the tissue-shrouded contents.

As the tissue paper fell away, she found herself staring at the paperweight snowstorm she had fallen in love with all those years ago.

She turned it upside down, then back again, and watched in delight as the snow began to fall softly around the old house standing serene and enchanted in its glass bubble.

Then, tears in her eyes and a wonderful smile on her lips, she rose and set it down carefully, before throwing her arms around Ross's neck. 'Thank you…' she said unsteadily. 'It's the most wonderful present I've ever had. I—I wish I knew what to say…'

'If you really want to please me, you could try saying, "I love you".'

Taking off the robe, she tossed it aside. 'Come to bed, and I'll show you.'

Laughing joyously, he swept her into his arms. 'That's the most gloriously wanton invitation I've ever had.'

Smiling up at him, the jewels at her throat and ears glittering in the firelight, she echoed his earlier words. 'Baby, you ain't seen nothin' yet.'

'And this is the woman who sounded so shocked when I suggested that three in a bed might be fun!'

Momentarily uneasy, she ventured, 'But you didn't mean it?'

'I most certainly did.'

As she looked at him wide-eyed, he carried her over to the shadowy four-poster and, setting her down carefully, turned back the bedclothes to reveal Onions, sleeping peacefully.

Straight-faced, he added, 'Of course, if you really *don't* like the idea of three in a bed…'

'Oh, I don't know… As you say, it might be fun.'

'I'll make sure it is,' he promised, and he started to strip off his clothes.

* * * * *

POSH DOCS

*Dedicated, daring and devastatingly
handsome—these doctors are
guaranteed to raise your temperature!*

**The new collection
by your favorite authors,
available in May 2009:**

**Billionaire Doctor,
Ordinary Nurse #53**
by CAROL MARINELLI

Claimed by the Desert Prince #54
by MEREDITH WEBBER

**The Millionaire Boss's
Reluctant Mistress #55**
by KATE HARDY

The Royal Doctor's Bride #56
by JESSICA MATTHEWS

HARLEQUIN Presents

International Billionaires

Life is a game of power and pleasure.
And these men play to win!

THE RUTHLESS BILLIONAIRE'S VIRGIN
by Susan Stephens

Rescued by the elusive, scarred billionaire
Ethan Alexander, Savannah glimpses the
magnificence beneath the flaws and gives
Ethan's darkened heart the salvation only
an innocent in his bed can bring....

Book #2822

Available May 2009

Eight volumes in all to collect!

www.eHarlequin.com   HP12822

NIGHTS *of* PASSION

One night is never enough!

*These guys know what they want
and how they're going to get it!*

UNTAMED BILLIONAIRE,
UNDRESSED VIRGIN

by Anna Cleary

Inexperienced Sophy has fallen for dark and
dangerous Connor O'Brien. Though the bad boy
has vowed never to commit, after taking Sophy's
innocence is he still able to walk away?

Book #2826

Available May 2009

Don't miss any of these hot stories, where sparky
romance and sizzling passion are guaranteed!

The Inside Romance newsletter has a NEW look for the new year!

Same great content, brand-new look!

The Inside Romance newsletter is a FREE quarterly newsletter highlighting our upcoming series releases and promotions!

Click on the Inside Romance link on the front page of
www.eHarlequin.com or e-mail us at
insideromance@harlequin.ca to sign up
to receive your FREE newsletter today!

You can also subscribe by writing to us at: HARLEQUIN BOOKS
Attention: Customer Service Department
P.O. Box 9057, Buffalo, NY 14269-9057

Please allow 4-6 weeks for delivery of the first issue by mail.

REQUEST YOUR FREE BOOKS!

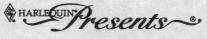 

2 FREE NOVELS
PLUS 2
FREE GIFTS!

YES! Please send me 2 FREE Harlequin Presents® novels and my 2 FREE gifts (gifts are worth about $10). After receiving them, if I don't wish to receive any more books, I can return the shipping statement marked "cancel". If I don't cancel, I will receive 6 brand-new novels every month and be billed just $4.05 per book in the U.S. or $4.74 per book in Canada, plus 25¢ shipping and handling per book and applicable taxes, if any*. That's a savings of close to 15% off the cover price! I understand that accepting the 2 free books and gifts places me under no obligation to buy anything. I can always return a shipment and cancel at any time. Even if I never buy another book, the two free books and gifts are mine to keep forever.

106 HDN ERRW 306 HDN ERRL

Name	(PLEASE PRINT)
Address	Apt. #
City	State/Prov.	Zip/Postal Code

Signature (if under 18, a parent or guardian must sign)

Mail to the **Harlequin Reader Service:**
IN U.S.A.: P.O. Box 1867, Buffalo, NY 14240-1867
IN CANADA: P.O. Box 609, Fort Erie, Ontario L2A 5X3

Not valid to current subscribers of Harlequin Presents books.

Want to try two free books from another line?
Call 1-800-873-8635 or visit www.morefreebooks.com.

* Terms and prices subject to change without notice. N.Y. residents add applicable sales tax. Canadian residents will be charged applicable provincial taxes and GST. Offer not valid in Quebec. This offer is limited to one order per household. All orders subject to approval. Credit or debit balances in a customer's account(s) may be offset by any other outstanding balance owed by or to the customer. Please allow 4 to 6 weeks for delivery. Offer available while quantities last.

Your Privacy: Harlequin Books is committed to protecting your privacy. Our Privacy Policy is available online at www.eHarlequin.com or upon request from the Reader Service. From time to time we make our lists of customers available to reputable third parties who may have a product or service of interest to you. If you would prefer we not share your name and address, please check here. ☐

HP08R